THREE EXEMPLARY NOVELS
With an Introduction

MIGUEL DE UNAMUNO

THREE
EXEMPLARY NOVELS

WITH AN INTRODUCTION BY ANGEL DEL RIO

TRANSLATED BY ANGEL FLORES

GROVE PRESS, INC.   NEW YORK

CONTENTS

INTRODUCTION

I cannot help wondering, rereading these three strange stories thirty-five years after their first publication, what will be the modern American reader's reaction to them. Their singularity was as great in 1920 as it is today, but it could more easily go unnoticed because their author was then widely recognized as the most important of contemporary Spanish writers, while today his name is less generally familiar. The *Three Exemplary Novels* seem, in their bareness, equally removed from actual experience as the raw material of literary creation and from current literary devices and fashions. But their relevance to the modern temper of anxiety and self-searching is perhaps greater than ever before. No matter how alien they may seem superficially to the prevailing taste, be it inclined toward violent naturalism or toward complex psychological probing, they still obviously deal with elemental forces of human personality, and they still convey, with their extreme, deceitful simplicity, the same sense of power that emanates from all of Miguel de Unamuno's works. For Unamuno, though a great writer and a great thinker, was above all a tremendously powerful and original personality.

No Spanish voice was heard during the fifty years of his active intellectual life which could compare with his in the strength of his passion nor in the profound seriousness with which he challenged every complacency, whether of literature, politics, or philosophy. He was primarily a nonconformist, a spiritual rebel in the tradition of the great heretics: a searcher for a truth that was not rational, but of that living sort which man has to find within himself.

Unamuno was known in European learned and literary circles, especially French and Italian ones, as early as 1913; the first English translation of his work, *The Tragic Sense of Life,* appeared in 1921. But his real prominence in America began in 1924, when one of the periodic eruptions of Spanish politics brought his name into the limelight. His defiance of Primo de Rivera's dictatorship, followed by his exile, made of him a sort of liberal hero. The Paris newspaper *Le Quotidien* arranged for his escape from the small Canary Island where he had been confined, and sent a boat to rescue him. Articles appeared about him in such publications as *The New York Times* and *The Literary*

Digest. Translations followed: the third story in the present volume appeared in *Best Continental Short Stories of 1924-25;* Knopf published in succession *Essays and Soliloquies,* the *Life of Don Quixote and Sancho,* and the novel *Mist.* Critics like Mark Van Doren, Eliseo Vivas, and Edwin Muir recognized Unamuno as a somewhat outlandish expounder of modern anxieties. His vogue increased in 1930 when, almost at the founding of the Spanish Republic, he returned triumphantly from exile.

Of greater literary significance were the appraisal of John Dos Passos in *Rosinante to the Road Again* (1922) and Waldo Frank in *Virgin Spain* (1926). Both Dos Passos and Frank had a lasting interest in Spanish culture and could not but be attracted to the man who was considered the greatest living figure of Spanish literature and so in the first rank of those whom Frank called "the awakeners." In the fields of religious and philosophical scholarship also Unamuno was admired. John A. Mackay, the present head of Princeton Theological Seminary, has acknowledged his debt to the Spanish thinker and has called him "Europe's most outstanding man of letters in the early decades of the present century." Warner Fite, author of *Moral Philosophy* and *The Living Mind,* a dissenter from the school of American pragmatism, wrote to a colleague: "I like him for his 'unbridled romanticism,' but above all because I can see in each page that Don Miguel knows very clearly what he is saying. His is a romanticism not of one who ignores the philosophy of schools, but of one whose soul has struggled at some moment with all its problems."

Of recent years, American interest in Unamuno has centered not so much on his political ideas and influence as on his search for a transcendent motivation in personal life and on his remarkable "Spanishness." William Jay Smith, reviewing a study of Unamuno recently in *The New York Times,* said of him: "No figure in modern literature has been more personal than Miguel de Unamuno, and yet there is no personality more difficult to define and assess. He himself disliked easy classifications: he was a philosopher and poet, a novelist and teacher, an essayist and political prophet, but above all, he was the incarnation of his country, one whose consciousness was 'a Spanish consciousness, made in Spain.' "

This characteristic of "Spanishness" in Unamuno, if over-emphasized, tends to obscure the larger and truer view of him as a writer who thought primarily of man as both personal and universal. He believed that by probing deeply the character of man belonging to a time and a place, one can discover what is universal and common to all men, what constitutes the brotherhood of the race. Nevertheless an analysis of Unamuno as the prototype of the Spaniard may furnish a key to his characteristic themes and literary devices, thereby deepening and enriching an understanding of *Three Exemplary Novels.*

Unamuno lived, as few men and writers have lived, in conflict and contradiction, and it is precisely this living in inner strife which constitutes the core of his thought, of his literary work, of his significance.

Contradiction in him had many roots. A voracious reader, he absorbed the whole legacy of Western thought, from the Bible and the classics (he was a Professor of Greek) up to the writings of his contemporaries. Besides the ancient languages he read in sixteen modern ones. When few Europeans cared about North American literature, Unamuno was familiar with William James, Emerson, Whitman, Oliver Wendell Holmes, and many less significant figures. He learned Danish expressly for the purpose of reading Kierkegaard in the original, and became under his influence a forerunner of existentialist thought. He assimilated the works of Rousseau and Ibsen, Carlyle and Leopardi, Flaubert and Mazzini, Kant and Hegel, as well as those of Protestant theologians from Luther to such moderns as Ritschl, Harnack, Troeltsch and others, not to speak of those tormented spirits and masters of personal and religious anxiety, like Pascal or De Sénancour, with whom, as with Kierkegaard, he felt a particular spiritual kinship. He had an astonishing capacity to absorb the substance of his reading, to turn ideas into personal experience and to use them in his constant search for a personal truth. As he explained in his essay *La ideocracia,* he hated the tyranny of ideas to which, under the influence of rationalism, Western culture had submitted for centuries. He himself proclaimed a new creed of "ideophobia": ideas were not to be worshipped nor followed blindly, but were to be spent, by using them as shoes are used; they were to be subordinated to and made a part of life, the basic reality. Not life in a general and abstract sense, but the life of each individual, each concrete man of flesh and bone, who in Unamuno's view, is the subject and supreme object of all philosophy.

What we have said thus far is, substantially, that Unamuno was a typical intellectual of his time: the decades between the eighteen-seventies and the nineteen-thirties. He has to be associated with that group of thinkers who, following the romantic impulse, revolted against reason in the name of life: Nietzsche, Kierkegaard, Bergson, the irrationalists, pragmatists and vitalists—intellectuals all of them, who, reaching a point of saturation, reacted for intellectual reasons against the intellect and intellectuality. What differentiates Unamuno from the rest of the group is that, thoroughly Europeanized as he was, he turned violently against the European tradition. He made of quixotism a new religion and preached a crusade to bring back the knight-errant of La Mancha to ransom the European soul from bondage to the cult of reason and material happiness. Taking pride in the fact that Spain was often considered a half-African country, he proclaimed the need to Africanize Europe.

In Unamuno, as in all public figures, there was undoubtedly a streak of exhibitionism; he enjoyed his role of dissenter. Nothing could better define his personality and thought than the title of one of his books: *Contra esto y aquello (Against This and That)*. On the other hand, there cannot be the slightest doubt that he was profoundly and dramatically sincere. To understand the basis of conflict in him we have to look further than that dualism of Being and Reason which he shared with his European contemporaries. The real source of Unamuno's significance as the incarnation of tragic contradiction is to be found in the structure of Spanish history. Contradiction and conflict have become part of the Spanish being, and Unamuno, well prepared for it by temperament and education, chose to make of it the center of his spiritual life.

Spain shares with other European countries the

great tradition of the West: Hebrew, Greek, Roman, Christian, the Germanic invasions. But she has had other historical experiences which set her apart. She experienced in the Middle Ages eight centuries of living contact with two great Semitic cultures, the Arab and the Jewish. She is the only modern European nation which has passed through a complete imperial cycle, having created and lost a vast empire. On the threshold of modern times she was the Defender of the Catholic Faith, the champion of the Counter Reformation. The result was, by the end of the sixteenth century, a deadly isolation from those main currents of European thought which carried the seeds of the great achievements of Western culture during the last three hundred years.

Thus the history of Spain became a permanent drama. On the one hand she could not renounce her European tradition. On the other she could not compromise, in the Age of Reason, the principles of the fighting Catholic Faith which had come to be the very root of her national character as well as the justification of her struggle against the stream of modern history. Since the eighteenth century

Spanish intellectual life has been characterized by the efforts of enlightened minorities to keep up with modern ideas and forms of life, while preserving the essential traits of the national spirit. A country divided, at odds with itself, Spain has lived for two centuries in a permanent state of civil war, violent at certain moments, concealed or repressed at others.

Unamuno's generation, the generation of '98, asserted itself by the intensity with which it felt this national discord. It was not composed of historians or political thinkers, but of artists and poets, highly subjective according to the literary climate of the moment. Each one expressed in his own way the dismal feeling of a fatherland in perpetual crisis, endeavoring at the same time to open new vistas for the future. Together they produced the highest literature to come out of Spain since the Golden Age. After the initial impulse, they followed different paths. Unamuno, more than any of the others, continued to identify himself with the tragic problem of Spain. By wrestling with the conflict of a whole nation he came to wrestle, as few other thinkers of our epoch have, with the

22

essential problems of life, of death, and of human existence.

He was a liberal, and for many years was considered a prophet of regeneration, but he carried the two Spains within him and felt at ease with neither. Thus he was the fiercest critic of the Monarchy; thus, though one of the fathers of the Republic, he soon turned against it to accept, though but for a few days, the rebels of 1936. Nothing could have been further from his spirit than the Franco regime, and he tried again, so far as circumstances permitted in those days of totalitarian terror, to shout his protest. So he died on the last night of that tragic year—in complete despair, we can but imagine, at the sight of his country's Cain complex unleashed in all its fury. He wanted a whole Spain, not a divided one, as in his writing he strove for the idea of the whole man.

While for the rest of the world Unamuno has therefore become the embodiment of the Spanish spirit, to many of his countrymen he is the incarnation of rebellion, of all that they consider negative and harmful to Spanish tradition. Not long ago, at the celebration of the seventh centenary of the

University of Salamanca, of which he was the most eminent professor and rector in modern times, the bishop of the diocese prohibited a homage that had been prepared for Unamuno. A number of Catholic authors now criticize him for the heretic quality of his thought—heretic, that is, from the point of view of Catholicism. And with reason, for Unamuno's religion, like everything else about him, was deeply personal. Perhaps no better description has been given of the roots of his inner conflict than that of Hernan Benitez in *El drama religioso de Unamuno:* he was a man of "a Protestant mind and a Catholic heart."

The *Three Exemplary Novels* are highly representative of Unamuno's conception of the tragic character and of his original and totally arbitrary idea of what a novel should be. Their conciseness as compared to his other works of fiction gives the reader a sharper view of his power to concentrate in elemental terms the assertiveness of human personality with its inner contradictions and conflicts. For the novel was to Unamuno chiefly a medium of expression for a philosophy which could not be systematized—a method of vitalizing thought. As he himself said, "reason annihilates and imagination completes, integrates or totalizes; reason by itself alone kills, and it is imagination that gives life."

The central idea in all his fiction is the struggle to create faith from doubt and ethics from inner strife. Life is a constant wrestling with mystery, a drama with two main characters: man and an ever-elusive God, i.e. elusive in terms of rational certainty. The essence of human personality he finds in a proposition of Spinoza's *Ethics:* "Everything, insofar as it is in itself, endeavors to persist in its own being." But men are mortal, and they cannot reconcile themselves to ignoring what is to become of them. They cannot reconcile their feeling of life, their urge for eternity, with the mystery of death. Faith gives them a solution: God, at least the Christian God, is the warrantor of eternity. But reason and science have destroyed the ground where Faith is born and grows. As a result, modern man is bound to live in doubt—not rational Cartesian doubt, but vital existential doubt. This is the root of what Unamuno calls "the tragic sense of life," because for him the impossibility of certainty is not a source of skepticism, pessimism or renunciation, but rather of energy for the constant quixotic strife. Life itself is nothing but that strife: man is forced to struggle in uncertainty and at the same time to seek after truth. This means that he is forced to live in "agony," an agony inherently tragic. "If it is nothingness that awaits us," he concludes, "let us make an injustice of it; let us fight against destiny, even though without hope of victory; let us fight against it quixotically."

For sheer power and for bareness of literary devices, *Three Exemplary Novels* can hardly be compared with anything currently in vogue. In structure and tone they are closer to drama than to any form of narrative literature. Their harshness and their stifling atmosphere of passion are reminiscent of some of the plays of Strindberg (a writer very much influenced by Ibsen, as Unamuno was in his youth) or of O'Neill. The significant difference is that Strindberg and O'Neill are naturalistic authors whose works are studies in hatred and lust, while Unamuno's aims are predominantly philosophical and metaphysical: he does not attempt to foster psychological understanding of human behavior but to give, as he would say, "glimpses of the deep mystery of man's soul and conscience." It is in this sense that his works are related to existentialist literature.

The three stories here included are typical of Unamuno. Their common elements are these: First, each has a central character or "agonist" endowed with a strong will and bound to subdue or destroy anyone who interferes with or opposes him. Secondly, these "agonists" are deficient in all moral and social conventionalism. Finally, the customary detailed treatment of atmosphere in space and time, without which it is indeed difficult to conceive what we call a novel, is almost entirely absent.

The driving passion in Raquel, the main character of "Two Mothers," and Carolina, the heroine of "The Marquis of Lumbria," is the maternal instinct. In the case of Raquel it is almost demoniac in its intensity; in Carolina it is mixed with other motives and is weaker but perhaps more complex. The dominant passion of Alejandro Gomez is not so clearly defined: it is pure will, the absolute affirmation of the *I*, the *self*, in complete alienation of the *you,* the others. Confronted with these three, minor characters are of no importance; they become either victims or mere puppets. Their weakness has sometimes been called a defect in Unamuno's fiction, but it must not be forgotten that it is a direct result of his concept of life. In the world of existence, of human will, either you *are* or you *are not.*

Thus conceived, character is stronger than any moral or social convention, for personality justifies itself. It obeys the method of passion, which Unamuno described many years before he wrote these tales:

Arbitrariness, the brusque affirmation of a thing because I wish it to be so, because I need it to be so, the creation of our vital truth—truth being that which makes us live—is the method of passion. Passion affirms, and the proof of its affirmation is founded upon the energy with which it is affirmed. When some poor intellectual, some modern European, opposes ratiocinations and arguments to any of my affirmations, I say to myself: reasons, reasons, and nothing more than reasons!

28

It is no wonder, then, that the author's protagonists have all the marks of abnormality, both in the pathological sense and in the sense of not conforming to type. But Unamuno's distinctive feature as a novelist is that he refrains from the slightest suggestion either of psychological analysis or of moralizing. He treats the abnormal as if it were absolutely normal. He condemns neither the unscrupulousness of Raquel and Carolina nor the frightful nature of Alejandro's love. He accepts them as they are. So, surprisingly enough, does the reader.

Unamuno's treatment of social background in these stories also puts them in a class of their own. He purposely avoids description. Nevertheless his characters do not move in a social vacuum. Spanish society in some of its less amiable aspects is deftly sketched, and a harsh view is taken of human relations, particularly domestic life. Parents sacrifice everything to interest. Berta's family accepts dishonor; Julia's swindler father does not hesitate to trade on his daughter's beauty. The home seems to be half prison, half insane asylum—a "diminutive hell" like the Count of Bordaviella's hearth. The aristocracy is represented by idle dissipaters, the easy prey of upstarts like Alejandro Gomez, or by weaklings living in a dismal world of the past.

Without impairing the tightness of his design, Unamuno has sharply delineated some typical themes in the Spanish literary tradition. For instance, "honor," the most powerful motif of Spanish classical drama and supposedly of Spanish social behavior, is treated with complete negativism. "Don Juanism" is caustically presented, whether in the case of Raquel's lover and victim, or in the Count of Bordaviella, that caricature of the professional lover. For Unamuno, playing with love is not a sign of masculinity but of weakness and effeminacy, which he contrasts with the whole woman absorbed by maternal passion or the whole man with his all-possessive love.

Less salient but still present in these stories is the theme of the Cain complex, which obsessed Unamuno and which he developed fully in one of his most tragic novels, *Abel Sançhez*. It represented for him the primitive impulse of human nature, the bedrock of personality vying for recognition. It is also, of course, the source of fratricidal war, a national disease in Spain. Here it is implicit in the general atmosphere of hatred, and becomes explicit in the story of Carolina and Luisa.

Unamuno repeatedly claimed that all truly original fiction is autobiographic, taking inner experience for its primary source. He "lived" the essential problems of human existence intensively, but he was at the same time a classicist and a scholar who found in the Bible and in Greek literature the first and perhaps the most universal exploration of the mystery of personality. Of the *Three Exemplary Novels* two deal with the theme of Rachel, Jacob's second and barren wife. Most of the elements freely combined and modernized in the two novelettes can be found in Genesis: "And when the Lord saw that Leah was hated, he opened her womb; but Rachel was barren"; "Give me children, or else I die"; "Behold my maid Bilhah, go in unto her; and she shall bear upon my knees, that I may also have children by her." What is new in Unamuno's stories, aside from the atmosphere, is the ruthlessness of both Carolina and Raquel. Maternity is not only the center of woman's nature but it is also related to one of the forms of immortality: immortality of the flesh, which Unamuno, in true Catholic fashion, could not conceive as separated from the spirit. The same idea is revealed with even greater intensity in the third story, with relation to Alejandro's fatherhood.

In this as in other respects, "Nothing Less than a Man" is the most powerful of the *Three Exemplary Novels*. It has become one of Unamuno's best known works, having been translated into several languages and successfully adapted for the stage. It is a typical example of "the tragic sense of life" and of the intensity of which Unamuno was capable. Alejandro Gomez is the quintessence of pure, raw masculinity. His name is significant: Gomez is the Spanish equivalent of Smith, and is reinforced by the quantitative and qualitative connotations of the name Alejandro. He has no lineage or ancestry: "My family?" he says to his wife. "I have no family but you. I am my family. I and you who are mine." He is not a product of society nor of history; the world is *his* world, the one that he creates. The real meaning of the novel is to be found not so much in his relation to his surroundings as in his encounter with love and death, the two moving forces of human existence. His love, like that of

Raquel or Carolina, destroys its own object. But Alejandro, unlike them, is confronted with his equal, a real woman, Julia, whose possessiveness is as great as his own. The tragic sense of the story lies in the fact that both fail. Julia gains the certainty of Alejandro's love only at the doors of death; Alejandro ends by destroying himself after having destroyed with Julia everything that mattered to him.

Alejandro Gomez is the embodiment of man's will deprived of spiritual strength. His struggle with death becomes in the last instance a struggle with God. He had never dared to look within himself. It is his failure in the face of love and death, the inscrutable designs of God, rather than his contempt for his fellow men, which gives him tragic dimensions. Thus, more than any other of Unamuno's fictional heroes, Alejandro enacts the author's central idea: the drama of individual life is the result of pure will, without horizons beyond the ambit of our conduct; we are condemned to live in agony.

THE MARQUIS OF LUMBRIA

THE large manorial house of the Marquis of Lumbria, "the palace" as it was called in the gloomy city of Lorenza, was like a chest of silent, mysterious memories. Although it was inhabited, its windows and balconies that faced the street were almost always closed. Its façade, which boldly displayed the great coat-of-arms of the Lumbria family, faced the south toward the spacious square of the Cathedral and stood opposite to this imposing baroque edifice; but since the sun shone upon it almost all day long, and there are scarcely any cloudy days in Lorenza, all its shutters remained closed. And this happened because the most excellent Marquis of Lumbria, Don Rodrigo Suarez de Tejada, abhorred sunlight and fresh air. "Street dust and sunlight," he used to say, "do nothing but dull the furniture and spoil the rooms—and then the flies . . ." The Marquis had a veritable horror of the flies which might come from a ragged, or perhaps a scurvy beggar. The Marquis trembled at the possibility of contracting any of the plebeian diseases. The people of Lorenza and its environs were so filthy . . .

The rear of the mansion faced an enormous rugged cliff that overlooked the river. A blanket of ivy covered the wide walls of the palace on this side. And though the ivy sheltered mice and other vermin, the Marquis respected it. It was a family tradition. And on a balcony, built here on the shady side, free from the sun and the flies, the Marquis used to sit down to read while the murmur of the river soothed him, as it rushed down the narrow channel of its bed, forcing its foaming course among the rocks of the cliff.

The most excellent Marquis of Lumbria lived
with his two daughters, Carolina, the elder, and
Luisa; and his second wife, Doña Vicenta, a
woman with a dull brain, who, when she was
not sleeping, was complaining of everything,
especially of the noise. For, just as the Marquis
feared sunshine, the Marquise feared noise; and
while the former went on summer afternoons
to read in the shade of the ivy-covered balcony
to the sound of the river's song, his wife stayed
in the front parlor and took her siesta in an old
arm-chair upholstered in satin which the sun
had not touched, lulled by the silence of the
Cathedral square.

The Marquis of Lumbria had no male children, and this was the most painful thorn in
his existence. Shortly after having become a
widower, he had married Doña Vicenta, his
present wife, in order to have a son, but she
had proved sterile.

The Marquis' life was as monotonous and

as quotidian, as unchanging and regular, as the murmur of the river below the cliff or as the liturgic services in the cathedral. He managed his estate and pasture lands, to which he paid short visits from time to time, and at night he used to play *ombre* with the priest, the intimate advisor of his family, a curate, and the clerk of records. They all arrived at the same hour, crossed the threshold above which was exhibited a plaque of the Sacred Heart of Jesus with its inscription: "I shall reign in Spain, more reverenced there than elsewhere," seated themselves around the little table already arranged for them, and on the stroke of ten, with the mechanical precision of a clock, they parted until the following day, even though there might still be open stakes. Meanwhile the Marquise dozed off and the Marquis' children did their needlework, read edifying books—perhaps some others not so pious, obtained by stealth—or quarreled with each other.

For in order to break the tedium which sat-
urated the whole house, from the parlor closed
tight against the sun and flies to the ivy clad
walls, Carolina and Luisa had to quarrel.
Carolina, the elder, hated the sun, like her
father, and kept herself rigorously observant of
all the family traditions; while Luisa liked to
sing, to peep out at the windows and even to
plant flowers in flower-pots—a vulgar custom
according to the Marquis. "Haven't you a
garden?" he said to his daughter, referring
to a tiny garden which adjoined the palace, but
was seldom visited by any of the latter's inhabi-
tants. But Luisa wanted to have flower-pots
on the balcony of her bedroom, which faced a
side street of the cathedral square; she wanted
to water them, and with this as a pretext, to
watch the passers-by. "What bad taste to pry
into what does not concern us . . ." her father
would say; and her older sister, Carolina,
added: "Not only that, but still worse to go

hunting for people!" And then the fun would begin.

And the ventures upon the bedroom balcony and the watering of the flowers yielded their fruit. Tristan Ibañez del Gamonal, of a titled family, one of the oldest in the city of Lorenza, remarked the second daughter of the Marquis of Lumbria; he saw her smiling, with her violet eyes and geranium mouth, among her flowers. And it happened one day as Tristan was passing through the narrow street, the water overflowing from the flower-pots dripped upon his head, and when Luisa exclaimed: "O, excuse me, Tristan!" he felt as if the voice of a princess imprisoned in an enchanted castle were calling him to succor her.

"Such things, my daughter," said her father, "are done formally and seriously. I will have no foolishness!"

"But what do you mean by that, father?" exclaimed Luisa.

"Carolina will tell you."

Luisa stood looking at her older sister and the latter said:

"It does seem to me, sister, that we, the daughters of the Marquis of Lumbria, should not carry on flirtations and strut about like peacocks on the balcony as women of the working class do. Is that what the flowers were for?"

"Let that young man ask to be admitted," pronounced her father, "and as I have nothing against him, everything will be arranged. How about you, Carolina?"

"I," said the latter, "do not object either."

And so Tristan entered the house as a formal suitor for the hand of Luisa.

The Marquise did not perceive this at once. And as the *ombre* session passed, the lady dozed in a corner of the drawing room; and near her Carolina and Luisa, knitting or making lace, whispered with Tristan, whom they were careful to leave never alone with Luisa but always with the two. In this respect the father was most vigilant too, though he did not mind, on the other hand, if Carolina sometimes received her future brother-in-law alone, for thus she could better instruct him in the customs and traditions of the family.

*   *   *

The card players, the domestics and even the townspeople who were intrigued by the mystery of the mansion, noticed that shortly after Tristan's admission into the house as the sweetheart of the second daughter of the Marquis, the spiritual atmosphere of the hieratic family seemed to grow more dense and shadowy. The Marquis grew more taciturn, his wife complained more than ever about the noise when there was less noise than ever. For the quarrels and disputes of the two sisters were more frequent and violent than before, but more silent. When one of them insulted or pinched the

other, as they met in the hall, it would be an
affair of whispers and smothered complaints.
Only once did Mariana, the old chamber-
maid, hear Luisa shouting: "Well, the whole
city shall know it! Yes, the whole city shall
know it! I shall go out on the balcony that
looks towards the cathedral square and shout
it to everyone!" "Be quiet," roared the voice
of the Marquis, and then followed an expression, so unheard in that house, that Mariana
fled in terror from the door at which she had
been listening.

A few days later the Marquis went away
from Lorenza and took his eldest daughter,
Carolina, with him. And during the time he
was gone Tristan did not appear at the house.
When the Marquis returned, he felt obliged
one night to give some explanation at the card
party. "The poor girl is not feeling well," he
said looking fixedly at the priest, "it's a case
of nerves that comes from constant quarrels,

trivial, of course, with her sister whom she really adores, and so I took her away to recuperate." Nobody answered a word.

Shortly afterwards, the marriage of Tristan Ibañez del Gamonal to the second daughter of the most excellent Marquis of Lumbria was celebrated *en famille*—decidedly *en famille*. Besides the immediate family no one attended it except the mother of the groom and the card players.

Tristan came to live with his father-in-law and the atmosphere in the mansion grew denser and still more tenebrous. The flowers on the bedroom balcony of the newly wedded girl withered for lack of care. The Marquise slept more than ever and the Marquis roamed about hermetically closed chambers, like a ghost, silent and taciturn. He felt that his life was ebbing away, and he clutched at it. He gave up the card parties, as his farewell to the world—if he ever lived in the world. "I have not the head for the game now," he told his

46

confidant, the priest, "I am distracted every minute and the game no longer amuses me. The only thing left is to prepare myself to die well."

One day he awoke with a paralytic stroke. He hardly remembered anything. But as he recovered, he seemed to clutch life with a more desperate tenacity. "No, I can't die until I see how the affair turns out." And of his daughter, who brought him his dinner to the bed, he inquired anxiously: "How are things? Will it take long?"

"Not much longer, father."

"Well, I am not going away, I cannot go until I see the new Marquis; because it must be a male, a male! We need a man here and if it is not a Suarez de Tejada, it will be a Rodrigo and a Marquis de Lumbria."

"That does not depend on me, father . . ."

"Well, that would be the last straw, daughter," and his voice trembled as he said it, "that after we have taken that madcap into our

family, he should not give us a Marquis . . .
Why I would . . ."

Poor Luisa wept and Tristan seemed a crimi-
nal and a servant at the same time.

The excitement of the poor man reached its
height when he learned that his daughter was
about to deliver. He trembled all over with
a feverish expectancy. "You require more care
than the woman in the other room," said
the doctor.

"When Luisa gives birth to the child," said
the Marquis to his son-in-law, "if it is a son,
a Marquis, bring him to me at once that I may
see him and then die in peace; bring him to me
yourself."

When the Marquis heard the cry, he sat up
in bed and stared at the door. Shortly afterwards Tristan entered, looking remorseful and
carrying the child well wrapped up. "Marquis?" the old man shouted the question.

"Yes!"

He leaned forward a little to examine the new-born babe; he gave it a shaky tremulous kiss, the kiss of death, and without even looking at his son-in-law, he fell back heavily upon the pillow, senseless. Without regaining consciousness he died two days later.

With black cloth, they draped the coat-of-arms on the façade of the house in mourning, and the black of the cloth soon began to fade in the sun which shone full force upon it all day long. An air of mourning seemed to descend upon the whole house to which the child brought no happiness.

Poor Luisa, his mother, was left so weak after childbirth that though she insisted on nursing her child at the beginning, she had to give it up. "A hired breast . . . ," she sighed. "Now, Tristan, a wet nurse will nurse the Marquis," she repeated to her husband.

Tristan had fallen into an indefinable sadness; he felt himself growing old. "I am like an appurtenance of the house, almost a piece of furniture," he used to say. And from the narrow street he used to gaze at the balcony of Luisa's bedroom—there were no longer any flower-pots there.

"Couldn't we again put some flowers on your balcony, Luisa?" he once ventured to ask his wife.

"In this house one flower is enough—the Marquis," she answered.

The poor man suffered because they called his son nothing but the Marquis. Shunning his home, he took refuge in the cathedral. Sometimes he left the house, not knowing where he was going. And what hurt him most was that his wife did not even try to discover where he went.

Luisa felt that she was dying, for life was dripping from her drop by drop. "Life takes its leave like a fine stream of water," she said, "I feel my blood grow thinner; my head is buzzing, and if I'm still alive, it's only because I am dying very slowly . . . And if I regret it, it is for his sake, for my little Marquis, only for him . . . How sad life is in this sunless house! I once thought that you, Tristan, would bring sunshine and liberty and happiness; but no, you have brought me nothing but the little Marquis . . . Bring him to me!" And she covered him with long, tremulous, feverish kisses. Although they spoke to each other, between husband and wife fell a curtain of frozen silence. They said nothing of what most tormented their minds and hearts.

When Luisa felt that the thread of her life was about to break, placing her cold hand on her son Rodrigo's forehead, she said to his father: "Take care of the Marquis! Sacrifice yourself for the Marquis! Oh, and tell her that I forgive her!"

"And me?" moaned Tristan.

"You? You don't have to be pardoned!"

The words fell like a death sentence upon the poor man. And shortly after hearing them, he was left a widower.

*   *   *

A young widower, master of a considerable fortune, that of his son the Marquis, and imprisoned in that large gloomy house shut against the sun, his memories being only a very few years old, already seemed to him as old as the ages. He passed the dreary hours on the balcony at the rear of the house, listening to the droning river. Soon he resumed the card parties. He spent long hours alone with the priest, going over, so it was said, the papers of the late Marquis and arranging his will.

But what gave the whole city of Lorenza something to talk about was the fact that after an absence of some days, Tristan returned to the mansion with Carolina, his sister-in-law, now his new wife. But didn't people say that she had become a nun? Where and how had she lived during those four years?

Carolina returned proudly, with an air of insolent defiance on her face. The first thing she did on returning was to order that the mourning draperies be removed from the family coat-of-arms. "Let the sun shine on it," she exclaimed, "let the sun shine on it and I have a mind to have it daubed with honey so that it will fill with flies." Then she ordered the ivy to be removed. "But Carolina," begged Tristan, "leave it as an antique!"

The little marquis immediately perceived an enemy in his new mother. He would not consent to call her "mama" in spite of his father's requests; he always called her aunt.

"But who told him I am his aunt?" she asked. "Perhaps Mariana?"

"I don't know, wife, I don't know," answered Tristan, "I don't see how, but around here people know everything."

53

"Everything?"

"Yes, everything. It seems that this house tells everything . . ."

"Well, we shall keep quiet."

Life in the mansion seemed to acquire a bitter, concentrated intensity. The married couple seldom left their room, in which Carolina kept Tristan. And so the little marquis was left to the mercy of servants, of a teacher who came every day to teach him how to read and of the priest who undertook to instruct him in religion.

The card parties were renewed; but during them, Carolina, seated near her husband, followed his plays and even coached him in them. They all noticed that she did nothing but look for opportunities to put her hand on his and that she was continually leaning on his arm. When the clock was about to strike ten, she said, "Tristan, the time is up." He did not venture out of the house without her, holding his arm and sweeping the street with a look of defiance.

* * *

Carolina's pregnancy was very painful. It seemed that she did not desire the child that was coming. Nor did she wish to see it when it was born. And when she was told that it was a girl born ill-formed and weak, she only answered dryly: "Yes, our punishment!" And a little later when the poor creature was dying, the mother said: "For the kind of life she would have had to endure . . ."

"You are very much alone," Carolina said one day, years afterwards, to her nephew, the little marquis, "you need a companion, some one to stimulate you to study; and so your father and I have decided to bring home a nephew, one who was left an orphan . . ."

The boy, who was then already ten years

old, with a tendency towards illness and brooding, remained pensive.

When the other one came, the intruder, the orphan, the little marquis was on his guard and the town did nothing but comment on the extraordinary occurrence. Everyone thought that since Carolina had not been successful in having children of her own, she had brought the adopted son, this intruder, to annoy and quarrel with the other, her sister's child . . .

From the very beginning the two children regarded each other as enemies, for if the one was haughty, the other was no less so.

"Well, what do you think," said Pedrito to Rodriguin, "that because you are a marquis you are going to give me orders? . . . If you annoy me much more I'll go away and leave you alone."

"Leave me alone, that's how I want to be. Go back to where your own folks are."

But Carolina would come in and with a

"Children!" make them look at each other in silence.

"Uncle," Pedrito would say to Tristan (he called him 'uncle'), "I'm going away. I want to go away. I want to go back to my aunts. I can't stand Rodriguin; he is always throwing it up to my face that I am here only out of charity and to serve him."

"Have patience, Pedrin, have patience. Haven't I?" And caressing the child's little head, he kissed it and shed copious tears, slowly and silently over him.

Those tears were for the child like a rain of pity. He felt a profound sorrow for the poor man, for the poor father of the little marquis.

Carolina was the one who never wept.

*   *   *

It happened one day, while husband and wife were lying close together on the sofa, staring vacantly into space, their hands clasped, that they heard the noise of a quarrel and suddenly the children burst in, sweating and breathless.

"I'm going away! I'm going away!" cried Pedrito.

"Go! Go! And don't come back to my house!" answered Rodriguin.

But when Carolina saw the blood on Pedrito's nostrils, she leaped towards him like a lioness shouting: "My son! My son!" And then, turning to the little marquis, she spat out this word: "Cain!"

"Cain? Is he my brother?" asked the little marquis opening his eyes widely.

Carolina hesitated a moment. And then, as if clenching her heart, she said in a harsh voice: "But he is my son!"

"Carolina!" groaned her husband.

"Yes," continued the little marquis, "I suspected that he was your son, and they say so around here . . . But what we don't know is who his father is . . . if he has any."

Carolina stiffened suddenly. Her eyes flashed, her lips trembled. She seized Pedrito, pressed him between her knees and looking fixedly at her husband exclaimed:

"His father? You tell him, you the father of the little marquis, you tell Luisa's son, you tell the grandson of Don Rodrigo Suarez de Tejada, Marquis of Lumbria, tell him who his father is! Tell it to him! Tell him! If you don't, I will! Tell him!"

"Carolina!" begged Tristan weeping.

"Tell him. Tell him who is the true Marquis of Lumbria!"

"You do not need to tell me," said the child.

"Well then, I shall! The marquis is this one and not you; he who was born before you and is my son, and who is the rightful heir, your father's son . . . yes, your father's . . . I shall remove the coat-of-arms and open all the balconies to the sun and I shall make everyone recognize my son for what he is: the Marquis."

Then she began to shout, calling all the servants and the old Marquise, who now almost in the imbecility of second childhood, was dozing. And when she had them all before her, she ordered the balconies opened wide and in a loud, calm voice she said:

"This, this is the Marquis; this is the true Marquis of Lumbria; this is the rightful heir. This is the son I had by Tristan, of this very Tristan who now hides and weeps, just after he had married my sister, a month after they were married. My father, the most excellent Marquis de Lumbria, sacrificed me to his principles—perhaps my sister was as much compromised as I myself . . ."

"Carolina!" groaned her husband.

"Be silent you—today I must reveal everything. *Your* son, yours and hers, has drawn blood, blue blood! no, just red blood, very red blood from *our* son, from my son, from the Marquis . . ."

"What a noise, good Heavens!" complained the old lady, cuddling up in an armchair in the corner.

"And now," continued Carolina addressing herself to the servants, "go and shout the news throughout the city: repeat what you have heard me say in the public square, in the court-yards and beside the fountains. Let everyone know of it—let them know of the blot on the escutcheon."

"Why all the city knew it already," mumbled Mariana.

"What?" shouted Carolina.

"Yes, madam, yes; every one said so . . ."

"And to keep a secret that was known, to conceal a mix-up that was clear to every one, to cover up appearances—for what have we lived like this, Tristan? Misery, nothing but misery! Open those balconies, let the light enter, all the light and dust and flies of the street, and tomorrow we shall take down the

61

escutcheon. We shall place flower-pots on all the balconies and a party will be given for the people of the city, the real people. But, no, the party will be given on the day when my son, your son, whom the priest calls a child of sin, when the real sin was the one which made the other one your son, shall be recognized for what he is—the Marquis of Lumbria."

They had to carry poor Rodriguin from a corner in the room—he was pale and feverish. Afterwards he refused to see either his father or brother.

"We shall put him in a school," Carolina decided.

*   *   *

Afterwards all Lorenza people spoke of nothing except the masculine firmness with which Carolina executed her plans. She went out daily, holding her husband by the arm as if he were her prisoner and holding the hand of their son. She kept all the balconies of the mansion wide open, and the sun faded the satin of the arm-chairs and even fell upon the ancestral portraits. Every night at the card game she received the guests who did not dare to refuse her invitations and she stayed at Tristan's side playing his cards. She caressed him before the guests and patting him on the cheek she would say to him: "My, what a man you are, Tristan!" And then to the others: "My poor, dear husband doesn't know how to play alone!" And when they had gone, she would say to him: " 'Tis a pity, Tristan, that we haven't more children . . . after that poor little girl . . . she was a daughter of sin, she, not our Pedrin; but now to bring up this one, the Marquis!"

She made her husband recognize Pedrin as his son, begotten before his father had married, and she began to prepare for her son the succession to the title. Rodriguin in the meantime, away, at school was being consumed with sadness and anger.

"The best thing that could happen," said Carolina, "would be for him to be inspired to a religious vocation. Haven't you ever felt such an inspiration, Tristan? For it seems to me that you were born more to be a monk than anything else . . ."

"And *you* say that, Carolina! . . ." her husband ventured to say in a supplicating tone.

"Yes, I really think so, Tristan! And don't pretend to be proud of what happened, what the priest called our sin and my father, the Marquis, called the blot on our escutcheon. Our sin? Not yours, Tristan, no. I was the one who seduced you! I! She, the girl of the geraniums, who watered your hat—your hat and not your head—with the water from her flower-pots, brought you to the house, but it was I who won you. Remember that! I wanted to be the mother of the Marquis. Only

64

I didn't count on the other one. And the other one, he was strong, stronger than I. I wanted you to rebel and you did not know how, you could not rebel . . ."

"But Carolina . . ."

"Yes, yes, I know well enough what happened; I know. Your flesh has always been weak. The sin was your letting him marry you to her: that was your sin. And what you made me suffer! But I knew that my sister, that Luisa, couldn't endure her betrayal and your infamy. And I waited. I waited patiently and reared my son. What a task it was to bring him up when a terrible secret divided us! I have brought him up for revenge! And as for you, his father . . ."

"Yes, he must despise me . . ."

"No, he doesn't despise you, no! Do you think I despise you?"

"Well, what then?"

"I pity you! You awoke my flesh and with

it my pride as the heiress. Since nobody could meet me except formally and through my father . . . since I didn't go peeping out upon the balcony as my sister and smile on the people in the street . . . since no men come here except farmers and card players . . . When you came here I made you feel that *I* was the woman, *I*, and not my sister . . . Do you want me to remind you of our sin?"

"No, for God's sake, Carolina, no!"

"Well, it's better that I shouldn't remind you of it. You're the fallen one. Do you see why I said that you were born to be a monk? But no, no, you were born that I might be the mother of the Marquis of Lumbria, of Don Pedro Ibañez del Gamonal y Suarez de Tejada. Him I shall make a man. And I will order him to carve himself a new escutcheon, made of bronze and not of stone. That's why I had the stone one removed to make room for a bronze one. On it will be a red stain, blood-red, blood-red like the blood which his brother, his step-brother, your other son, son of sin and betrayal, drew from him, red as my blood, red as the blood which you too made me shed . . . Don't grieve," and as she said this she touched his head, "don't feel depressed, Tristan, my husband . . . Look here, look at my father's portrait and tell me, you who saw him die, what he would say if he saw his other grandson, the Marquis . . . So he made you carry your son, Luisa's son, to him! I shall place a ruby on the bronze escutcheon, and the ruby will sparkle in the sun. Well, did you think that there was no blood, red blood, red and not blue, in this house? And now, Tristan, as soon as we see our son, the red-blooded Marquis, asleep, let us go to bed."

Tristan bowed his head under the weight of centuries.

TWO MOTHERS

1

How Raquel weighed on poor Don Juan!
The widow with the torture of being left childless—a torture that penetrated the heart of her
soul—had seized him in her clutches and kept
him to an unchanging mode of life. In Don
Juan will had died with desire. Raquel's eyes
and her hands lulled and calmed all his appe-
tites. And that solitary home, illegitimately
established, was like the cell of a pair of lovers
in a monastery.

Lovers? Was he, Don Juan, in love with
Raquel? No, merely absorbed by her, sub-
merged in her, lost in the woman and in her
widowhood. For Raquel, so Don Juan thought,

was, above everything else, a widow and a
childless widow at that; Raquel seemed to have
been born a widow. Her love was a violent
love that savored of death, that searched within
her man, so very deep within him, that it
emerged from him like something beyond life.
And Don Juan felt himself dragged by her into
the lower depths of earth.

"This woman will kill me," he would say
to himself, and saying it he thought how sweet
would be that everlasting rest in the earth's
bosom, after having been killed by a widow like
her.

For some time Raquel had been coaxing her
Don Juan into matrimony—into getting married, but not to her, as the poor man would
have liked to do.

RAQUEL. Marry me? But that, sweetheart,
is senseless! . . . What for? Why should we
marry according to the Church and the Civil
Law? Marriage, according to what we were

taught in the Catechism, was established for the purpose of wedlock, to give God's blessing to married people and to have them bring up children for His glory. We marry? Why, we're pretty well married already! Bless us? Alas, monkey—and as she said this she passed the five very delicate fingers of her right hand over his nose—now neither you nor I can gain blessing even with benedictions. To bear children for His Kingdom . . . to bear children for His Kingdom! . . .

With these words, her voice faltered and on her lashes trembled liquid pearls in which the fathomless blackness of her eyes was reflected.

DON JUAN. But I have already told you, Quelina, that there's one thing we can do, that is to get married as God and man command . . .

RAQUEL. You, my dear little monkey, invoking God?

DON JUAN. To get married that way, according to law, and adopt a child . . .

RAQUEL. Adopt a child! . . . Adopt a child! Why didn't you add—from the Orphan Asylum?

DON JUAN. Oh, no! that little nephew of yours, for example . . .

RAQUEL. I have already told you, Juan, not to speak of that . . . never to mention it again . . . My sister, since we are well off . . .

DON JUAN. That's right, we are . . .

RAQUEL. Of course it's right! Or perhaps you think that I don't know that your fortune, as well as everything else that's yours, belongs only to me, entirely to me?

DON JUAN. Entirely to you, Quelina!

RAQUEL. My sister would let us have any one of her children, I know; she would gladly give us one. And since it would cost me nothing to obtain it, I could never consider it my own. Oh! not to be able to have a child—have a child, and die in childbirth!"

74

DON JUAN. Please don't go on this way, darling.

RAQUEL. It's you, Juan, it's you who ought not to go on that way . . . An adopted child, a child we can adopt, is always like an orphan from the Orphan Asylum. Become a father, Juan, become a father since you have not been able to make me a mother. If you could have made me a mother, we would have been married . . . in that case, yes . . . Why do you lower your head that way? Of what are you ashamed?

DON JUAN. You are going to make me cry, Raquel, and I . . .

RAQUEL. Yes, I know, it's not your fault— it was not my husband's either, he . . .

DON JUAN. And now that! . . .

RAQUEL. All right! But you can give me a child. How? By begetting it upon another woman, a child of yours, and then letting me have it afterwards. Whether she likes it or not, I want it so and that's enough!

DON JUAN. But how can you want me to love another woman?

RAQUEL. Love her? What's this about loving her? Who said anything to you about loving another woman? I know well enough that at the present time you could not love another woman even if you wanted to. Nor would I consent to it! But it is not a question of loving her, it is a question of making her pregnant! Is that clear? It is merely a matter of making her a mother. Make her a mother and then give me the child, whether she likes it or not.

DON JUAN. Any woman who would lend herself to such a thing would be a . . .

RAQUEL. With *our* money?

DON JUAN. And to what woman shall I propose this?

RAQUEL. Propose what?

DON JUAN. That . . .

RAQUEL. What you are to propose to her is marriage . . . Yes, Juan, yes; marriage! You must get married and I shall find the woman for you; a woman who offers the possibility of success . . . And who is good-looking, eh?

As she said this she laughed; her laugh sounded like a sob.

RAQUEL. She will be your wife, and of course I can't be jealous of your wife . . .

DON JUAN. But she will be jealous of you . . .

RAQUEL. Naturally! And that will aid our plan. You will marry, you will be blessed, many times with a great many blessings, and you will have at least one child . . . for me. And I shall take it to heaven.

DON JUAN. Don't blaspheme . . .

RAQUEL. Do you know what heaven is? Do you know what hell is? Do you know where hell is?

DON JUAN. They say that it is in the center of the earth.

RAQUEL. Or perhaps in the center of a sterile womb . . .

DON JUAN. Raquel! . . . Raquel! . . .

RAQUEL. Come, come here . . .

She made him sit down upon her firm thighs, she pressed him to her bosom like a child and, bending her dry lips to his ear, she said in a half-whisper:

RAQUEL. I have already found a wife for you . . . I have already chosen the one who is to be the mother of our child . . . No one has ever searched for a wet-nurse with greater care than I have that mother . . .

DON JUAN. And who is she? . . .

RAQUEL. Señorita Berta Lapeira . . . But, why are you trembling? Why, I even thought that you would be pleased. What is it? Aren't you pleased? Why are you so pale? Why are you crying so? Weep, weep my child . . . Poor Don Juan!

DON JUAN. But Berta . . .

RAQUEL. Berta is thrilled. And not because of *our* money, no! She is in love, desperately in love with you . . . And Berta, who has the heroic heart of a virgin in love, will accept the rôle of redeemer, of saving you from me, for I am, according to her, your eternal damnation and your hell. I know it! I know it! I know how Berta pities you . . . I know the horror which I inspire in her . . . I know what she says about me . . .

DON JUAN. But her parents . . .

RAQUEL. Oh, her parents, her most Christian parents, are very reasonable parents . . . And they realize the importance of *your* money.

DON JUAN. Our money . . .

RAQUEL. They, like all the rest, think that it is yours . . . And isn't it legally yours?

DON JUAN. Yes, but . . .

RAQUEL. Yes, we must arrange even that carefully. They do not know how you are mine, my pet, and how everything you possess is mine and mine only. And they don't know how the child that their daughter will give you will be mine . . . Because you will have one, won't you darling? You will have a child? And at this point her words so excited Don Juan that they made him almost dizzy.

RAQUEL. You will have one, Juan, you will have one?

DON JUAN. You're going to kill me, Raquel.

RAQUEL. Perhaps . . . But first give me the child . . . Do you hear? There you have the angelic Berta Lapeira, Angel! Ha . . . ha . . . ha . . .

DON JUAN. And you, a devil! . . .(shouting, standing up and struggling to remain so.)

RAQUEL. The devil is also an angel, darling.

DON JUAN. But a fallen angel . . .

RAQUEL. Then make Berta fall; make her fall!

DON JUAN. You are killing me, Quelina, you are killing me . . .

After this, Raquel had to go to bed. And later, when Don Juan went to lie beside her, when he touched his lips to those of his mistress, he found them parched and burning like the sands of the desert.

RAQUEL. Now dream of Berta and not of me. Oh no, no! Dream of our child!

Poor Don Juan could not dream.

II

How had it occurred to Raquel to propose Berta Lapeira as his legitimate wife? How had she discovered not that Berta was in love with him, with Don Juan, but that he, when he was asleep and beyond the power of that will which was not his own, but Raquel's, dreamed that that angelic creature might come to aid and redeem him? And if there was a spark of future love in this, did Raquel mean to extinguish it by having him marry her in order to make the sterile widow a mother?

Don Juan had known Berta from childhood. Their families had been friends for many years. The parents of Don Juan, left a lonely orphan at a very early age, had been great friends of Don Pedro Lapeira and his wife. They had always been interested in Don Juan and had grieved more than any one else over his dissipations and his affairs with chance adventuresses. Therefore, when the poor man—wrecked by love-affairs, not by love—sighted the port of the sterile widow, they rejoiced at the good fortune of their friend's son, without suspecting that that port was a stormy one.

Contrary to what Don Juan believed, the judicious Lapeiras looked favorably on that relationship which was indeed a sort of wedlock, for Don Juan needed a will to make up for the one he lacked, and if the pair finally came to have children, their friends' son would be saved. They spoke frequently about this at

82

dinner time, during their intimate chats about the town's tragi-comedy, without being cautious in front of their daughter, the angelic Berta, who consequently became interested in Don Juan.

But Berta, when she heard her parents lamenting the fact that Raquel had not borne a child to Don Juan and that soon that fortuitous union might be secured forever before all human and divine law—or rather, before all theocratic and democratic law—felt within herself the wish that this might not be so, and then when she was alone, she dreamed of becoming the redeeming angel of that man shipwrecked by his loves and of lifting him from the stormy port.

How did it happen that Don Juan and Berta had had the same dream? Once, during the frequent visits that Don Juan made to the Lapeira house when their eyes met, as they shook hands, that dream had been born. And perhaps it might even have happened that it was Berta who received her childhood companion and that her parents were somewhat late in coming in.

Don Juan foresaw the danger, and, governed by Raquel's will, which was his, visited that house less frequently. The Lapeiras guessed the cause of his absence. "She certainly has him trained. She keeps him away from everyone!" the parents said to each other. And to their daughter, the angelic Berta, a little fallen angel whispered, speaking to the ear of her heart in the silence of the night and of dreamland: "He fears you . . ."

And now it was Raquel, Raquel herself, who was pushing him into Berta's lap. Into her lap?

Poor Don Juan missed the stormy high-seas of his former passing love affairs; he had a presentiment that Raquel was leading him to death. Why, he had no desire at all for paternity! . . . Why should he give another like himself to the world?

But what could he do? . . .

And again, impelled and guided by Raquel, he frequented the Lapeiras. His visits cheered the hearts of the girl and her parents. And more so when they divined his intentions. They began to pity him more than ever because of the fascination under which he lived. Don Pedro and Doña Marta commented upon it.

DON PEDRO. Poor fellow! It's quite evident that he's suffering . . .

DONA MARTA. Any one would suffer, Pedro, under such conditions . . .

DON PEDRO. Our Tomasa, do you remember? used to attribute it to a love-potion . . .

DONA MARTA. Well, that was funny about the love-potion . . . If the poor devil had only seen herself in a mirror . . .

DON PEDRO. And if she could have seen how she looked after nine childbirths and all that hard work . . . And if she could have seen how nice her rival looked . . .

DONA MARTA. That's what you men are like . . . all pigs . . .

DON PEDRO. All of us?

DONA MARTA. Excuse me, Pedro, not you! You . . .

DON PEDRO. But, after all, anyone could understand that little widow's love-potion . . .

DONA MARTA. Ah, you rascal, so . . .

DON PEDRO. I have eyes in my head, Marta, and eyes are always young . . .

DONA MARTA. Younger than us . . .

DON PEDRO. And what would become of this fellow now?

DONA MARTA. Allow him to come, Pedro . . . Because I can see he'll be coming . . .

DON PEDRO. And I too! But how about her?

DONA MARTA. I'll get her ready in case . . .

DON PEDRO. And that love-affair?

DONA MARTA. But don't you see, my dear

86

man, that he's trying to break it? Don't you
see that?

DON PEDRO. Undoubtedly. But a break like
that must cost him some sacrifice . . .

DONA MARTA. And even if that's so . . . He
has plenty, plenty, and although he should sacrifice something . . .

DON PEDRO. That's true . . .

DONA MARTA. We must redeem him, Pedro;
his parents demand it of us.

DON PEDRO. And we must make our daughter demand it, too.

The latter, on her part, was extremely
anxious for Don Juan's redemption. Don Juan's
or her own? She said to herself: "To snatch
away this man and see what her man is like,
the man she made, the man who has surren-
dered himself to her, body and soul . . . What
she must have taught him! . . . What my poor
Juan must know! . . . And he will make me
like her . . ."

The person with whom Berta was madly in love was Raquel. Raquel was her idol.

III

Poor Juan, now without the "Don," trembled between the two women, between his angelic and his demonic redeemer. Behind him was Raquel and before him Berta, and both were driving him on. Where to? He saw that it was toward perdition. He would lose himself in them. Between the two they were tearing him apart. He felt like that baby for whom two mothers were pleading before King Solomon, only he did not know which of them, Berta or Raquel, wished him to be kept whole for the other and which one wished to cleave him asunder. The clear blue eyes of the maiden Berta, like a fathomless, shoreless sea, summoned him to an abyss; and behind him, or rather, around him, enveloping him, were the black shadowy eyes of the widow Raquel, like an infinite, starless night, driving him on towards the same abyss.

BERTA. But what is the matter with you, Juan? Unburden your grief to me. Am I not your childhood friend, almost your sister? . . .

DON JUAN. Sister . . . sister . . .

BERTA. What is it? Don't you like that—sister? . . .

DON JUAN. I never had one; why, I hardly knew my mother . . . I cannot say that I have known any woman . . .

BERTA. You can't, eh? Come, now . . .

DON JUAN. Women . . . yes! But a woman, a real woman, no!

BERTA. But that widow—Raquel?

Berta was surprised that she uttered this without any violence whatsoever, without a tremor in her voice, and that Juan listened with absolute calm.

DON JUAN. That woman, Berta, has saved me; she has saved me from women.

BERTA. I believe you. But now . . .

DON JUAN. Now, yes; now I must save my-self from her.

And as he said this, Juan felt that a glance from the somber eyes of the widow was push-ing him on more violently.

BERTA. Can I help you to do that in any way? . . .

DON JUAN. Oh, Berta, Berta . . .

BERTA. Oh, come now, why evidently you want me to be the one to propose . . .

DON JUAN. But Berta . . .

BERTA. When are you going to feel that you're a man, Juan? When will you have a will of your own?

DON JUAN. All right, then,—do you want to save me?

BERTA. How?

DON JUAN. By marrying me!

BERTA. Will we ever understand each other —you wish to marry me?

Don Juan. That's clear!

Berta. Clear? Not so clear! Do *you* wish to marry me?

Don Juan. Yes!

Berta. Of your own will?

Juan trembled as he became aware of the pitch darkness in the depths of the maiden's clear blue eyes. "Can she have guessed the truth?" he said to himself, and was on the verge of retreating, but the widow's black eyes urged him on, saying: "Say what you said you would, you cannot lie . . ."

Don Juan. Of my own free will!

Berta. But, Juan, have you a will?

Don Juan. It is to acquire one that I wish to make you my wife . . .

Berta. And then . . .

Don Juan. And then, what?

Berta. Are you going to leave this other woman first?

Don Juan. Berta . . . Berta . . .

BERTA. Well, then, we won't say anything more about that, if you prefer. For all this only means that you, feeling that you are incapable of ridding yourself of that woman, want me to be the one to rid you of her. Isn't that so?

DON JUAN. Yes, it is so. (And he lowered his head.)

BERTA. And you want me to give you the will you lack . . .

DON JUAN. That is true . . .

BERTA. And to struggle against her will . . .

DON JUAN. Yes, that . . .

BERTA. Then, so it shall be!

DON JUAN. Oh, Berta . . . Berta! . . .

BERTA. Don't move. Look at me but don't touch me. My parents may appear at any moment.

DON JUAN. And they, Berta?

BERTA. But, Juan, are you really so simple not to have discovered that we had foreseen and discussed this matter already . . .?

DON JUAN. Then . . .

BERTA. We will all gather to save you.

IV

The arrangement for his wedding with Berta poisoned the very foundations of poor Juan's soul. Berta's parents, the Lapeiras, insisted upon having their daughter's economic future well secured and protected against all contingencies. At the same time, perhaps, they were thinking of their own. She was not, as some people believed, an only child—there was also a son who had fled to America at a very early age and was never spoken of again, especially in his own home. The Lapeiras endeavored to make Juan give Berta a dowry before taking her as his wife, and they, on their part, refused to give their future son-in-law an account of the state of their fortune. And Juan, in turn, refused the dowry, affirming that immediately after his marriage, he would make

93

a will in which he would name his wife as the sole inheritor of his property, after having set aside a small sum—and his future parents agreed upon this—for Raquel.

Raquel offered no obstacle either to the Lapeiras or their daughter. They agreed to live on friendly terms with her, as with an intelligent friend who had been in a certain way Juan's savior. Both parents and daughter were confident that the latter would know how to win her husband's heart completely with gentleness and cunning, and that, in the end, Raquel herself would contribute to the happiness of the newly-weds. Provided, of course, that they would assure her the mode of life and the respect which well-off, decent people are entitled to. She was not, after all, a vulgar adventuress nor one who had ever sold herself to the highest bidder. Her affair with Juan was an act of pure passion, of pity perhaps— the Lapeiras thought, or liked to think so.

But the serious part of the business, which neither the parents of the angelic Berta nor anyone in the city—and they claimed that they knew the widow!—could foresee, was that Raquel had made Juan sign a deed by which all his real estate appeared to have been bought by her, and all the other valuables which he possessed were made over in her name. Poor Juan seemed to be merely her administrator and agent. And all this the astute woman knew how to keep a secret. And all along she knew better than anyone the condition of the Lapeira fortune.

RAQUEL. Just think, Juan, within a short time, perhaps before you are married, or at any rate a little while after your wedding, the small fortune of Berta's parents, the fortune of your future spouse . . . spouse, eh? . . . not wife . . . spouse! . . . the fortune of your future spouse will be mine . . . or rather, ours . . .

DON JUAN. Ours?

RAQUEL. Yes, it will be for the child we're going to have, that is if your wife gives us one . . . And if not . . .

DON JUAN. You are killing me, Quelina . . .

RAQUEL. Keep still, my pet. I have my hands on that fortune already. I am going to buy up their notes and mortgages. Oh, yes! after all, that Raquel is a good soul, a real lady, she has saved the man who is to be our daughter's husband, she has preserved us from ruin, she is the shelter of our old age! And that she will be—of course she will! Why not?

DON JUAN. Raquel! . . . Raquel! . . .

RAQUEL. Don't groan like that, Juan, don't bleat like a lamb being slaughtered . . .

DON JUAN. That's what this is . . .

RAQUEL. No, it is not! I'm going to make a man of you! I'm going to make you a father!

DON JUAN. You?

RAQUEL. Yes, I, Juan! I, Raquel!

(Juan felt the pangs of death.)

DON JUAN. But tell me, Quelina, tell me (and he said this with sobs in his voice), why did you fall in love with me? Why did you make me lose my head with passion for you? Why have you sucked from me the marrow of my will? Why have you made me a puppet? Why didn't you let me lead the life I was leading? . . .

RAQUEL. By this time, having ruined yourself, you would be dead from misery and corruption!

DON JUAN. It would be better so, Raquel, better! Dead, yes; dead from misery and corruption. Isn't this misery? Isn't this corruption? Am I my own master? Am I, myself? Why have you stolen my body and soul?

Poor Don Juan was choking with sobs.

Once more, as she had done before, Raquel took him in her arms, like a mother, seated him on her lap, caressed him, pressed him to her sterile bosom, against her breasts, full of red blood that could not be changed into white milk, and bending her head to his, covering his ears with her loosened, disheveled hair, she wept and sighed over him. And she said to him:

RAQUEL. My child, my child, my child . . . I didn't steal you; it was you who stole my soul, you, you. And you stole my body . . . My child . . . my child . . . my child! . . . I saw you lost, lost, lost . . . I saw you looking for what cannot be found . . . And I was looking for a child . . . And I thought I should find one in you. And I thought that you would give me the child for which I am dying . . . And now I want you to give it to me . . .

DON JUAN. But, Quelina, it will not be yours . . .

RAQUEL. Certainly it will be mine, mine, mine . . . Just as you are . . . Am I not your woman?

DON JUAN. Yes, you are my woman . . .

RAQUEL. And she will be your wife. Woman!—as the shoemakers say: "My Woman!" I will be your mother and the mother of your child . . . of my child . . .

DON JUAN. And if we do not have one?

RAQUEL. Be still, Juan, be still! If you do not have one? If she does not give us one . . . I would . . .

DON JUAN. Raquel, keep still, the hoarseness of your voice frightens me!

RAQUEL. Yes, and then . . . afterwards . . . I would marry you to another woman!

DON JUAN. And if it's my fault . . .?

Raquel pushed him abruptly away from her. She stood up suddenly as if she had been struck and fixed her penetrating gaze on Juan; but soon the icy chill passed from her heart, she opened her arms to her man shouting:

RAQUEL. No, come to me, come to me, Juan! My child! My child! Why should I want another child? Are you not my child?

And she had to put him to bed—he had fallen into a feverish faint.

v

No, Raquel did not consent to attend the wedding as Berta and her parents desired, nor did she have to feign illness as an excuse—she really was ill.

RAQUEL. I never thought, Juan, that they'd go so far. I was well aware of the conceit and presumption of the girl and her parents, but I didn't think they were prepared to defy social conventions like that. To be sure, our relations have been in no way scandalous, for we have never appeared in public bragging about them; but they are more or less well known through the whole city. And in insisting that you should invite me to the wedding they're only trying to make their daughter's triumph more evident. Imbeciles! And she? Your wife?

DON JUAN. For God's sake, Raquel, you must . . .

RAQUEL. What? How is she? How are her embraces? Have you taught her some of what you learned from other women? For you could never teach her anything of what I taught you! How is *your* wife? You . . . you are not hers . . .

DON JUAN. No, nor am I my own . . .

RAQUEL. You are mine, mine, mine, darling, mine . . . And now you know where your duty lies. Then be sensible about it. And come to our house as infrequently as possible.

DON JUAN. But, Raquel . . .

RAQUEL. Raquel does not count. Now you belong to your wife. Take care of her!

DON JUAN. Why she herself advises me to go to see you occasionally . . .

RAQUEL. I knew. The little fool! She has even begun to imitate me, hasn't she?

DON JUAN. Yes, she imitates you as much

as she can: in her dress, in the way she combs
her hair, in her gestures, in her carriage . . .

RAQUEL. Yes, when you came to see me the
first time, on that almost formal visit, I noticed
that she was studying me . . .

DON JUAN. And she says that we ought to
become more intimate, since we live so near, so
very near each other, almost side by side . . .

RAQUEL. That's her diplomacy in trying to
substitute for me. She wants you to see us together often so that you may compare . . .

DON JUAN. I think it's something else . . .

RAQUEL. What?

DON JUAN. That she has taken a fancy to
you, that you dominate her . . .

Raquel lowered her gaze to the floor, her face
had suddenly become intensely pale, and she
raised her hands to her breast, pierced by a stab
of pain. And she said:

RAQUEL. We must make all that bear
fruit . . .

As Juan bent down to take his good-bye kiss
—the moist, long, full-mouthed kiss of former
times—the widow repulsed him, saying:

RAQUEL. No, not now! I don't want you
to take it to her, nor do I wish to take hers from
you.

DON JUAN. Jealous?

RAQUEL. Jealous? You fool! Do you think,
darling, I could be jealous of your wife. . .?
Of your wife? I, your woman? . . . For wedlock, to give God's blessing to married people
and to have them bring up children for God's
kingdom! For heaven and for me!

DON JUAN. You are my heaven . . .

RAQUEL. Sometimes you say your hell . . .

DON JUAN. That's so.

RAQUEL. Come here, come here, my child,
take this . . .

She took his head between her hands, gave
him a dry, burning kiss on his forehead and said
to him in parting:

RAQUEL. Now go and do your duty by her. And fulfill your promise to me. If you don't, you know, I would . . .

VI

It was true that Berta was studying from Raquel the way to win over her husband, and at the same time the way to win over Raquel herself, the way to be like her, to be a woman. And so she allowed herself to be absorbed by Juan's mistress, and kept discovering herself through the other woman. At last, one day when she could no longer resist—it was the time when the two of them, Raquel and Berta, had sent their Juan on a hunting trip with some friends—his wife went to see the widow.

BERTA. You must be astonished to see me here, alone like this . . .

RAQUEL. No, I'm not astonished . . . I even was expecting a visit from you . . .

BERTA. Expecting it?

RAQUEL. Yes, of course. After all, it seems to me that I've done something for your husband, for our good Juan, and perhaps the marriage . . .

BERTA. Yes, I know that if you, with your friendship, had not saved him from women . . .

RAQUEL. From women . . . Bah!

BERTA. And I appreciate your generosity . . .

RAQUEL. Generosity? What in? Ah, yes, I see what you mean . . . But no! No! How was I to hold him to my fate? For he did, in fact, want to marry me . . .

BERTA. I supposed so . . .

RAQUEL. But as we had already tried, the parson's benediction, even if he had married us and blessed us, would not have made it possible for us to have children . . . Why are you blushing so, Berta? Haven't you come to talk to me openly, heart to heart? . . .

BERTA. Yes, yes, Raquel, speak that way to me!

RAQUEL. I could not sacrifice him to my self-ishness. What I have not accomplished, may he accomplish!

BERTA. Oh, thanks, thanks!

RAQUEL. Thanks? No, no thanks! I have done it for him!

BERTA. Well then, for having done it for him . . . thanks!

RAQUEL. Oh!

BERTA. Are you astonished?

RAQUEL. No, I am not astonished, but you'll soon learn better . . .

BERTA. Learn what? To pretend?

RAQUEL. No, to be sincere!

BERTA. Do you think I'm not?

RAQUEL. There are very sincere pretensions. And marriage is their school.

BERTA. And how is that?

RAQUEL. I once was married!

BERTA. Ah yes, to be sure, you're a widow!

RAQUEL. A widow . . . A widow . . . I was

always one . . . I think I was born a widow
. . . My real husband died before I was born
. . . But let's stop this madness and raving!
How do you get along with Juan?

BERTA. Men . . .

RAQUEL. No, the man, the man! When you
told me that I had saved our Juan from women,
I shrugged my shoulders. And now I tell you,
Berta, you must take care of the man, of your
man. You must seek the man in him . . .

BERTA. I try to do that, but . . .

RAQUEL. But what?

BERTA. I fail to find any will in him . . .

RAQUEL. And you've come to look for it
here, perhaps?

BERTA. Oh no, no! But . . .

RAQUEL. You'll never get anywhere with
those "buts" . . .

BERTA. Where should I get?

RAQUEL. Where? Do you want me to tell
you where?

Berta, intensely pale, hesitated, while the steely eyes of Raquel seemed to crack the silence. And finally:

BERTA. Yes. Where?

RAQUEL. Become a mother! That is your duty. I have not been able to be one—that remains for you!

There was another oppressive silence, which Berta broke, exclaiming:

BERTA. I'll become one!

RAQUEL. Thank God! Didn't I ask you whether you came here to look for Juan's will? Well, the will of our Juan, of our man, is just that—to become a father!

BERTA. His?

RAQUEL. Yes, his. His, because it is mine!

BERTA. Now I admire your generosity more than ever . . .

RAQUEL. Generosity? No, no . . . And always count on my true friendship which may be useful to you yet . . .

BERTA. I don't doubt it . . .

And as they said good-bye, accompanying her to the door, she said:

RAQUEL. Ah, and tell your parents that I must come to see them . . .

BERTA. My parents?

RAQUEL. Yes, a matter of business . . . To console myself for my widowhood I devote myself to business, to financial enterprises . . .

And after shutting the door, she murmured: "Poor woman!"

VII

When at last, one autumn morning, Berta announced to her husband that he was going to become a father, he felt the two chains which kept him prisoner painfully rubbing against the flesh of his soul. He began to feel the weight of his dead will. The great combat had come. Was the child really to be his? Was he going to be a father? What was it like to be a father?

Berta, on her part, was in transports. She had conquered Raquel! But she felt that the victory was at the same time a defeat. She remembered the widow's words and her sphinxlike glance as she uttered them.

When Juan brought the good news to Raquel, she grew deathly pale, she almost ceased to breathe, then her face glowed, she gasped for breath, beads of perspiration appeared and she had to sit down; finally, in a dreamy voice, she murmured:

RAQUEL. At last I have you, Juan!

And she hugged him and pressed him madly to her palpitating body, she kissed his eyes and his lips, and then held him off at arm's length with the palms of her hands against his cheeks, gazing into his eyes, into those eyes that reflected her, like a mirror, so small . . . and she kissed him again. She gazed fixedly at her own tiny image, reflected in his eyes, and then, as if out of her senses, she muttered in a hoarse voice: "Let me kiss myself!" and she covered his eyes with kisses. And Juan thought he was going crazy.

RAQUEL. And now, now you can come here more often than before . . . Now you do not need her so much . . .

DON JUAN. Nevertheless, now is the time when she most wants me near her . . .

RAQUEL. That may be so . . . Yes, yes, now she is becoming . . . That's so . . . You must surround the poor little thing with affection . . . But soon she will get tired of you . . . you will be in her way . . .

And so it was. The first few months Berta liked to have him near her and feel his caresses. She passed hour after hour with her hand over Juan's, gazing into his eyes. And without wishing to, she spoke to him of Raquel.

BERTA. What does she say about this?

DON JUAN. She was overjoyed to learn of it . . .

III

BERTA. Do you think so?

DON JUAN. Why shouldn't I? . . .

BERTA. Well, I don't! That woman is a demon . . . a demon who has fascinated you.

DON JUAN. And not you?

BERTA. What kind of love potion has she given you, Juan?

DON JUAN. Again the same old story . . .

BERTA. Now you will be mine, mine only . . .

("Mine! Mine!" thought Juan, "that's what they both say!")

BERTA. We must go to see her!

DON JUAN. Now?

BERTA. Yes, now, right now. Why not?

DON JUAN. To see her, or to have her see you? . . .

BERTA. To watch her seeing me! To see how she will look at me!

Berta made her Juan take her for a walk, and she hung on his arm, seeking people's glances. But some months after, when it was

112

painful for her to move about there occurred
what Raquel had predicted—her husband's
presence upset her and she sought to be alone.
The period of nausea and vomiting began and
sometimes she would say to her Juan: "What
are you doing, you, what are you doing here?
Go on, go and take a walk in the fresh air and
leave me alone . . . What a pity it is that you
men do not experience these things! . . . Get
out of here, you, get out, I'm sick . . . Won't
you be quiet? Why must you move that chair
around . . . No, no! don't paw me! Go out!
I'm going to bed! Go out and don't come back
for a long while! Go on! Go on and see her,
and talk about my suffering . . . I know, I
know well enough that you wanted to marry
her, and I know why she didn't want you for
a husband . . ."

Don Juan. What are you saying, Berta? . . .

Berta. Why, she told me so, herself, she
who is after all a woman, a woman like me . . .

Don Juan. Not like you! . . .

Berta. No, not like me! She has never gone through what I am going through now . . . And you men are all pigs . . . Go on, go to see her . . . Go to see your widow . . .

And when Juan went from his house to Raquel's and told her what his wife had said to him, the widow was almost mad with joy. And again she covered his eyes with kisses. She kept him with her. Sometimes she kept him all night, and at dawn, when she opened the door for him so that he might slip outside, she said after a last kiss: "Now that she does not wait for you, go to her, go and console her with fine words . . . And tell her that I have not forgotten her and that I am waiting . . ."

VIII

Juan walked up and down the room like one in a trance. He felt the emptiness weigh upon his head and heart. Berta's cries and groans came to him as from another world. He did not see señor Lapeira, his father-in-law, seated in a dark corner awaiting the arrival of his grandchild. And since poor Juan thought he was dreaming, he was not surprised to see the door open and Raquel enter the room.

"You?" exclaimed Don Pedro, getting up.

RAQUEL. Yes, it's I! I have come to see if I can't help in some way . . .

DON PEDRO. You? You to help at this critical moment?

RAQUEL. Yes, to go and fetch something or somebody . . . You know, something or other . . . Don't forget, Don Pedro, I'm a widow . . .

DON PEDRO. A widow, yes; but . . .

RAQUEL. No "buts"! I'll stay here!

DON PEDRO. All right, I'll go and tell my wife . . .

And presently one heard the following conversation between Raquel and Doña Marta.

DOÑA MARTA. But, for God's sake, Señora . . .

RAQUEL. Why, am I not a good friend of the family?

DONA MARTA. Yes, yes! but don't let her know . . . , don't let her hear you . . .

RAQUEL. And if she does hear me, what of it?

DONA MARTA. In God's name, Señora, speak lower . . . don't let her hear you . . . lower . . .

At that moment a piercing cry was heard. Doña Marta ran to her daughter's side, and Raquel stood listening to the silence that followed the cry. Then she sat down. And in a little while, when Juan passed by her, she stopped him by seizing his arm and asked him anxiously: "What is it?"

DON JUAN. A girl . . .

RAQUEL. Her name will be Raquel!

And the widow disappeared.

IX

At the conference with his parents-in-law, the grandparents of the new-born baby girl, Juan was greatly surprised that when he suggested, completely terrorized and with the widow's eyes boring through his back to his heart, that his daughter should be named Raquel, the Lapeiras raised no objection whatsoever. They seemed crushed. What had happened to them?

DONA MARTA. Yes, yes, we owe so much to that lady, so much . . . and, after all, she has been a mother to you . . .

DON JUAN. Yes, that's true . . .

DONA MARTA. And furthermore, I think she ought to be asked to be godmother to the little girl.

DON PEDRO. Especially since that will stop people's detestable talking . . .

DON JUAN. They won't say anything more, now that . . .

DON PEDRO. No! One must face public gossip. Especially when it is false. Or is it that if we should do this, you couldn't walk through the streets with your head erect?

DON JUAN. Yes, of course!

DON PEDRO. Well then, everyone after his own conscience.

And Don Pedro looked at his wife like one who has just uttered a profound truth that elevates him in the eyes of the one who should know him best.

And still greater was the surprise—which inspired actual terror in Don Juan—when he heard that Berta had answered sadly to the proposition of everything to the name and the godmotherhood: "Just as you wish!" The fact was that the poor woman, as a consequence of great losses of blood, seemed transported to a dream-world. With the incessant buzzing in her head everything seemed to be enveloped in mist.

After a short time, Raquel, the godmother,

all but installed herself in the house and began
to take care of everything. The new mother
saw her approach and looked upon her as a
phantom from another world. The eyes of
the widow shone with a new brilliancy. She
approached the young mother and gave her a
kiss which, although it was silent, filled the
room with its sound. Berta was tortured in
her sleep by a painful dream. She heard the
widow's voice, firm and positive, like a mistress to her servant, saying:

RAQUEL. And now, Berta, we must find a
wet-nurse. Because it does not seem wise to me
that in your present state you should want to
nurse the child yourself. That would endanger
both lives . . .

Berta's eyes filled with tears.

RAQUEL. Yes, I understand, it's very
natural. I know what motherhood means . . .
but prudence comes first . . . You must
save yourself for the future . . .

BERTA. But, Raquel, even if I die . . .

RAQUEL. Die? Who? The child? My Quelina? No, no . . .

And she went over to the baby and took it in her arms and began to swathe it, and then to kiss it with such frenzy that the poor new mother felt her heart melt in her bosom. Not being able to stand the nightmare, she groaned:

BERTA. That's enough, Raquel, enough, enough . . . Don't disturb her . . . What the poor little thing needs is sleep . . . to go to sleep . . .

And then Raquel began to rock and embrace the child, singing songs to her, in a strange tongue unfamiliar to Berta and to her family, as well as to Juan. And a heavy silence fell around those lullabies that seem to come from a distant world, far distant, lost in the mists of dreams. And Juan, hearing them, felt sleepy, but with the sleep of death, and a terrible dread filled his empty heart. What was all that?

What did it all mean? What did his life
mean?

X

Some time later, when Berta had recovered
her health and was beginning to awake from
the painful dream of childbirth, and saw herself
separated from her little daughter, from her
Quelina, by Raquel and by the wet-nurse whom
Raquel had found and who obeyed her in
everything, she knew that there would be a
struggle. At last she saw clearly the deep
abyss into which she had fallen; at last she
saw for whom and for what she had been
sacrificed. Of course she did not see everything, she could not see everything. There
were abysses in the widow which she, Berta,
could never succeed in reaching. Nor did she
attempt to, for only to peer over them made
her dizzy. And then those lullabies in that
strange tongue.

BERTA. But what are you singing to her?

RAQUEL. Oh, recollections of my childhood . . .

BERTA. What do you mean?

RAQUEL. Don't ask to know more, Berta. Why should you . . .?

No; she, Berta, could not want to know more! She knew too much already! Would that she did not know so much! If only she had not let herself be tempted by the serpent to taste the fruit of the Tree of Knowledge— of good and evil! And her parents, her good parents, seemed to have fled from the house. Their little granddaughter had to be taken to them for them to see her. And it was the wet-nurse who took her to her!

Then it was that Berta felt a consuming pity for her husband, her poor Juan, kindled in her heart. She would enfold him in her thin arms as if to protect him from some hidden enemy, from some terrible danger, and leaning her feverish, disheveled head on her husband's shoulder, she would weep and weep and weep, while her breast, heaving with convulsive sobs, would beat against the sorrowing heart of her poor Don Juan. And on one of these occasions, when the wife and mother had sobbed: "My child! My child! . . . My child! . . ." she was struck nearly dead with terror to see the death-like agony that convulsed and blanched Juan's face.

BERTA. My child, what's the matter with you? What's the matter?

DON JUAN. Be quiet, Quelina, be quiet . . . you are killing me . . .

BERTA. But Juan, you are with me, with me, with your Berta . . .

DON JUAN. I know not where I am.

BERTA. What is the matter, my child . . .?

DON JUAN. Don't say that . . . don't say that . . . don't say that . . .

Berta guessed the whole torment of her husband. And she resolved to conquer it, to adopt it, and to rescue him from it. Even if in doing so it might be necessary to abandon and give up her daughter. She wanted her man, her man!

And he, the man, Juan, on his part was feeling more and more like a man, a man rather than a father. He felt that he was no more than a means, an instrument for Raquel. An instrument for what? For satisfying a gnawing hunger for motherhood? Or rather, a strange vengeance, a vengeance of other worlds? Those weird lullabies in an unknown tongue that Raquel sang to Quelina, her daughter not her godchild—her own daughter, the widow's— didn't they speak of a sweet vengeance, of a gentle, drowsy vengeance, like a poison that puts one to sleep? How Raquel regarded him, her Juan, now! She sought him less frequently than before.

But when she did seek him and they met,

their meetings were like those of old, but more gloomy and more frenzied.

RAQUEL. And now (she said to him once) devote yourself more to your Berta, to your wife, give yourself more to her. You must give her a son, for she deserves one, because this child, my Quelina, is mine, mine, mine. And you know—she owes her birth to me, I owe her to myself. I almost made your Berta, our Berta, give birth to her upon my knees, as the Bible tells us. Now give yourself to her, my child!

DON JUAN. You are killing me, Raquel.

RAQUEL. Look here, Juan, you've sung that little refrain to me many times and I'm sure you've also repeated it to your wife at one time or another. Well, if you want to kill yourself, kill yourself, but don't blame us for it. But I really think you ought to live, for you have still many things to give Berta in this world.

And as Juan struggled to free himself from

Raquel's impetuous embrace, the latter, still
holding him, said:

RAQUEL. Yes, I've foreseen this—let her see
us . . . let her see us!

Berta entered.

RAQUEL. I saw *you*, Berta (and she stressed
the *you*), I saw *you* coming.

And throwing her arms like a yoke around
Juan's neck, and stepping a bit away from him
afterwards, she continued:

RAQUEL. But you are mistaken, I was courting your husband for you, winning him for
you. I was just telling him to give himself to
you, to give himself unreservedly. I yield him
to you. Since he has already made me a
mother, let him make you a mother. So that
you can call him "child" openly. That is, if
by this calling him "child" we are not, as he
says we are, killing him. You must know the
story of the two mothers who appeared before
King Solomon claiming the same child. And

here is the child . . . Don Juan of old! I don't want to cut him in two, for that would probably kill him, as he says. Take him whole.

BERTA. So, you . . .

RAQUEL. I am the real mother, I!

Then Berta, aghast, seized her husband, who let himself be pulled by the arm and, tearing him from Raquel's yoke, she turned to her and cried out:

BERTA. No, never! I am the mother, I, I, I . . . I love him whole, I love him whole even more than you do. Take him and finish him! But give me my daughter, give my child back to me!

RAQUEL. What child?

BERTA. My . . . my . . . my . . .

The name burned her lips.

RAQUEL. My Quelina? Who is I, myself . . .! I should give myself up? I give you my Quelina, my Raquel, so that you can make of her another Berta Lapeira, another like you?

Like all of you, honorable women? Alas, I was a wife too, yes, a wife; I know, too . . .

BERTA. But is it my fault that neither your husband nor Juan could do with you what Juan has been able to do with me, what I have been able to do with him?

RAQUEL. And you, Juan, you, *my child*, are you going to be divided? Or are you going to remain whole for your wife?

Juan fled from both of them.

XI

Juan fled from both of them, and he did more. How did it happen? It is only known that having gone out on a drive towards the Sierra, in an automobile, he was brought back to his home dying and he died at home without regaining consciousness. Neither the chauffeur nor the friend who accompanied him could explain very clearly what had occurred. As they

128

were passing along the edge of a narrow ravine they saw him disappear from the car—they could not say whether he fell or threw himself out—they saw him roll down the precipice, and when they reached him, he was beyond help. His skull was fractured and his body badly mangled.

What a look passed between Raquel and Berta over the motionless, white body of their Juan!

BERTA. Now the question of the child, my daughter, is clear . . .

RAQUEL. Clear? What is she going to live on? Who is going to support her? Who is going to educate her? And how? And you, what are you going to live on? How are your parents going to exist?

BERTA. And how about Juan's fortune?

RAQUEL. Juan left no fortune whatsoever . . .! Whatever there is is mine! And if you didn't know it before, you know it now!

129

BERTA. Thief! Thief! Thief!

RAQUEL. Those are mere words, and you don't know who has robbed whom. Maybe you're the thief . . . all of you, people in your position. I don't want you to make my Quelina, my daughter, a thief like yourselves . . . And now talk it over with your parents. See if it would suit you better to live like beggars, or on peaceful terms with a thief . . .

BERTA. Peaceful terms?

RAQUEL. Yes, at least in the eyes of the world!

* * *

Berta discussed the matter at great length with her parents, the Lapeiras, and the three of them, with a famous, reputable lawyer, examined Don Juan's will. He seemed to possess nothing of his own: Raquel had full power over his fortune. Finally they accepted the compromise. Raquel would support them and, in exchange, they were to give her the child.

The only consolation was that Berta might again become a mother, and that Raquel would set aside a small amount of money in the name of the posthumous son or daughter of poor Don Juan. But how was this unfortunate creature to be brought up?

RAQUEL. If you marry again (Raquel said to Berta) I will give you a dowry. Think it over. It is not well to remain a widow.

NOTHING LESS THAN A MAN

Julia's beauty was famed throughout the countryside that bordered the ancient town of Renada; Julia was, one might say, its official beauty, one more monument—but a living and fresh one—amid all the architectural treasures of the capital. "I'm going to Renada," people would say, "to see the cathedral and to see Julia Yañez." An omen of impending tragedy dwelt in the eyes of this beauty. Her demeanor was a source of uneasiness to all who knew or saw her. Old men grew sad when she passed by, compelling all eyes to follow in her wake, and young men would be long in falling asleep on those nights. And she, fully conscious of her power, sensed the weight of a fatal future hanging over her. A secret voice from the depths of her consciousness seemed to be saying: "Your beauty will undo you!" And she tried not to hear it.

The father of this local beauty, Don Victorino Yañez, a man of a rather shady past, had placed his last hope of economic salvation in his daughter. He was now engaged in business, but things were going from bad to worse. His last and supreme financial hope, the last card left for him to play, was his daughter. He also had a son; but he was a good-for-nothing and for a long time they had had no news of him.

"Julia is all that is left to us now," he used to say to his wife. "Everything depends upon the kind of a marriage she makes or we make for her. If she makes one foolish mistake, and I'm afraid she will, we're lost."

"And what do you call making a foolish mistake?"

"That's a fine thing for you to ask! I tell

you, Anacleta, you haven't a bit of common
sense . . ."

"Well, I can't help it, Victorino. You're the
only sensible person around here, so explain it
to me."

"Well, what you have to do, and I've told
you so a hundred times, is to watch over Julia
and prevent her from getting into those silly
love affairs in which the young girls around
here waste their time, lose their chances and
even their health. I want no little love chats
at the window, no sentimental stuff; no little
students for lovers."

"But what can I do with her?"

"Indeed! Make her understand that our
future, our mutual welfare, even our honor
perhaps,—you understand? . . ."

"Yes, I understand."

"No, you don't understand! Our honor—
you hear me?—the family honor depends upon
her marriage. She must keep herself desirable."

137

"Poor little child!"

"Poor little child? She absolutely must not throw herself into the arms of silly lovers, and she must not read those crazy novels, which only turn her head and fill it with air."

"But what do you want her to do about it?"

"Think things over carefully; she must realize what she can do with her beauty and take advantage of it."

"Well, when I was her age . . ."

"Come now, Anacleta, that's enough foolishness! You never open your mouth but out comes nonsense. You, at her age . . . You, at her age . . . Indeed! Don't forget that I knew you then . . ."

"Yes, unfortunately . . ."

And the parents of the beauty would leave each other only to begin a similar conversation the following day.

Poor Julia, fully comprehending the horrible purpose behind her father's calculations, suffered in consequence. "He wants to sell me," she would say to herself, "to save his bankrupt business; possibly to keep himself out of jail." And that was the truth of the matter.

Instinctively rebellious, Julia accepted the advances of the first admirer that came along.

"For heaven's sake be careful, my child," said her mother. "I'm well aware of what's going on. I have seen him strolling near the house and making signs to you. I know that he has written you a letter and that you have answered it . . ."

"What of it, mama? Must I live like a captive slave, till the day when some Sultan appears to buy me from my father?"

"Don't say such things, my child . . ."

"Can't I have a sweetheart like other girls?"

"Of course, but he must be a serious one . . ."

"How is one to know if he is serious or not? One must begin somewhere. You have to get to know a person before you can love him."

139

"Love him . . . love him. . . ."

"Why no, I suppose I must wait for my purchaser."

"One can't do anything with you or with your father. That's the way the whole Yañez family is. Ah! I rue the day when I was married . . ."

"That's just what I don't want to have to say some day.

And then her mother would let her alone.

Determined to risk everything Julia found the courage to go down to the first floor and speak to her lover from the window of a sort of little store. "If my father discovers us here," she thought to herself, "he would do something terrible to me. But it might be better so: people will then know that I am a victim whose beauty he wishes to barter." She came down to the window and, in this first interview, she confided to Enrique, a budding provincial Don Juan, all the miserable, gloomy details of her

home life. He had come to save her, to redeem her.

But Enrique, in spite of his infatuation with
the beautiful girl, felt his enthusiasm waning.
"This little wench," he said to himself, "puts
on tragic airs; she reads sentimental novels."
And once all Renada had been informed of
how this famous local beauty had permitted
him to approach her window, he began to seek
a way out of his compromising situation. He
found one soon enough. One morning Julia
came downstairs all upset, with her brilliant
eyes red from weeping and said to him: "Enrique, I can't bear this any longer. This is no
home nor family: this is hell. My father has
found out about our affair. He beat me last
night just because I was trying to defend myself—think of that!"

"What a brute!"

"You can't imagine what he is! And he said
that you would have him to deal with."

"We'll see—let him come! That's the last straw!" But, at the same time, he was saying to himself: "This really must stop; this ogre is quite capable of any atrocity if he sees his treasure being carried off, and since I can't get him out of debt . . ."

"Tell me, Enrique, do you love me?"

"What a question to ask me now!"

"Answer me; do you love me?"

"With all my heart and soul, darling!"

"But do you really?"

"Really and truly!"

"Are you ready to do anything for me?"

"Yes, anything!"

"Well then, come on, take me away. We must go away, but far, very far away, where my father won't be able to reach us."

"Compose yourself, little girl!"

"No, no, take me away; if you love me, take me away. Steal this treasure from my father so that he won't be able to sell it! I don't

want to be sold—I want to be taken away!"
And so they set about arranging their escape.

But on the following day—the one which they had appointed for the elopement—while Julia was ready with her little bundle of clothes impatiently awaiting the arrival of the carriage which had been secretly ordered, Enrique failed to put in his appearance. "Coward! Worse than coward! Despicable! Worse than despicable!" cried poor Julia, as she flung herself down on the bed and bit the pillow in her rage. "And he said he loved me! No, no, he did not love me; he loved my beauty. Indeed, not even that! What he wanted was to able to boast before all Renada that I, Julia Yañez—no less than I—had accepted him as a sweetheart. And now he'll go telling everyone how I offered to run away with him. Oh! Despicable, despicable, despicable! He is as mean as my father; despicable as all men are!" And she fell into an inconsolable despair.

"My child," said her mother, "I see that this affair is now over with and I thank God for it. But look here, your father is right; if you continue like this you will only bring discredit upon yourself."

"If I continue how?"

"Like this—accepting the advances of the first man who comes along. You'll acquire the reputation of being a coquette and . . ."

"So much the better, mother, so much the better! That way more men will present themselves. Especially so long as I have not lost what God gave me."

"Alas, alas! You are indeed your father's daughter, my child."

In fact, a little while after this, Julia accepted another suitor. She confided exactly the same things to him, and frightened him just as she had Enrique. But Pedro was of stouter heart.

And following the same preliminary steps,

she finally proposed to him her idea of running away.

"Look here, Julia," replied Pedro, "I don't object to our running off together. Why, you know I would be delighted. But after we have fled, where shall we go and what shall we do?"

"We shall see about that later!"

"No, we can't put it off. We must decide that now. As for me, at the present time and for some time to come, I won't be able to support you. I know that they won't admit us at my house and as for your father . . ."

"What! You don't mean to retreat, do you?"

"But what are we going to do?"

"You're not going to be a coward, are you?"

"What shall we do, pray tell me?"

"Well . . . commit suicide!"

"Julia, you're crazy!"

"Yes, I am crazy; crazy with despair, crazy with disgust, mad with horror at this father of mine who wants to sell me . . . And if you

were crazy and madly in love with me, you
would commit suicide with me."

"But, Julia, remember that you want me to
be so madly in love with you as to commit
suicide with you; you do not say that you would
kill yourself with me because you are madly in
love with me, but rather because you are crazed
by your disgust for your father and your home.
It is not quite the same thing."

"Ah! how well you reason! Love doesn't
reason!"

They, too, broke off their relations. And
Julia would say to herself, "He didn't love me
either, any more than the other one did. They
fall in love with my beauty, not me. I defy
them all!" Then she would weep bitterly.

"You see, my child," said her mother, "didn't
I tell you so? Another one gone!"

"A hundred of them, mama, a hundred, until
at last I find my own, the one who will deliver
me from you both. Oh, to want to sell me!"

"Tell that to your father."

And Doña Anacleta would go to her own room to cry all by herself.

Finally, Julia's father said to her, "Look here, my child, I have overlooked these two love affairs of yours, I have not resorted to the measures I should have taken. But I warn you now that I will not tolerate any more foolishness. Now then, you know my stand."

"Well, there's still more!" cried Julia in a tone of bitter irony, with a challenging look into her father's eyes.

"What is it?" he asked menacingly.

"It's that I have another sweetheart."

"Another one! Who?"

"Who? I'll bet you can't guess!"

"Come now, don't joke, answer me, for you make me lose patience."

"Well, no less a personage than Don Alberto Menéndez de Cabuerniga."

"What an outrage!" exclaimed her mother.

Don Victorino turned pale without uttering a word. Don Alberto Menéndez de Cabuerniga was an exceedingly wealthy landowner, dissolute, very capricious as regards women, and it was said of him that he did not spare any expense to win them. He was married but separated from his wife. He had already married off two of his mistresses and had given splendid dowers to both women.

"What have you to say to this, father? Are you silent?"

"That you are quite mad."

"I'm not mad nor do I see visions. He walks up and down our street constantly and watches our house. Shall I tell him that he is to arrange matters with you?"

"I'm going. If I don't this interview will end badly."

Her father got up and left the house.

"But my child! My child!" her mother remonstrated.

148

"Mother, I can assure you that this proposition doesn't strike him as being so very bad; I tell you that he is capable of selling me to Don Alberto."

The poor girl's will was wearing out. She realized that even a sale would be a redemption. The essential thing was to leave home; to escape from her father by no matter what means.

*   *   *

About this time an "Indian" (a Spaniard who has made his fortune in America), Alejandro Gomez, purchased one of the richest and largest estates on the outskirts of Renada. No one was certain about his origin nor his past life, for no one had ever heard him speak of his parents, his relatives, his home or his childhood. The only thing they knew about him was that his parents had taken him first to Cuba when he was very young and later to Mexico, where

(and no one knew just how) he has amassed
an enormous, a fabulous fortune—it was said
to run into several million dollars—before he
had reached the age of thirty-four, at which
time he had returned to Spain with the inten-
tion of settling there. People said that he was
a childless widower and told the most fantastic
legends about him. Those who had dealings
with him thought him ambitious, filled with
vast projects, strong willed, obstinate and self-
centered. He boasted that he was a plebeian.

"One can do everything with money," he
would say.

"Not always, and not every one can," people
would reply.

"Not every one, no; but those who have
known how to make money can. Of course
one of these would-be *señores* who inherits his
money—a sugar paste count or duke—can't do
anything, in spite of the millions he may
have. But I! I! I who have known how to

make my fortune myself by the strength of my arm? I?"

And you ought to have heard him pronounce the word "I." The whole man was concentrated in this personal affirmation.

"Nothing that I have really wanted to have I ever failed to obtain. If I wanted to I could become Prime Minister. But the fact is that I don't desire it."

* * *

People spoke to Alejandro of Julia, the monumental beauty of Renada. "We must see her," he said to himself. And as soon as he had seen her he exclaimed, "We must have her!"

One day Julia said to her father, "This fabulous Alejandro—you know the man; for a long time now they've talked of nothing else—the man who purchased the Carbajedo estate? . . .

151

"Yes, yes, I know who he is. Well, what about him?"

"Do you know that he, too, has his eye on me?"

"Julia, are you trying to make fun of me?"

"I'm not joking. I'm quite serious about it; he's courting me."

"I tell you not to joke . . ."

"Well, here's his letter!"

She took one from her bosom and thrust it into her father's face.

"And what do you intend to do?" he asked her.

"Indeed! What should I do? I'll tell him to arrange matters with you and that you will fix the price."

Don Victorino looked sharply at his daughter and left the room without a word. An ominous silence and an atmosphere of mute anger reigned throughout the house for a few days. Julia had written her latest suitor a sarcastic

and disdainful answer. Shortly after she received a reply containing the following words
heavily underlined and written in large, clear,
angular characters: "You will eventually be
mine. Alejandro Gomez knows how to get
what he wants." As she read this, Julia thought,
"Here is a real man. Will he save me? Will
I save him?" A few days after the arrival of
the second letter Don Victorino closeted himself with his daughter and said to her with tears
in his eyes and almost upon his knees:

"Listen, my child, now everything depends
upon your decision: our future and my honor.
If you refuse to accept Alejandro it will not
be long before I shall be unable to conceal my
ruin, my frauds and even my . . ."

"Don't tell me."

"No, I will no longer be able to hide anything. My terms are expiring. They will
throw me into prison. Until now I have been
able to ward off the blow because of you, by

bringing in your name! Your beauty has been my protection. 'Poor little girl,' they say."

"And if I accept him?"

"Well, then, I'll tell you the entire truth now. He has learned all about my situation, he has been informed of everything. And now, thanks to him, I breathe freely. He has settled all my bad debts and he has paid my . . ."

"Yes, I know, don't tell me. But what now?"

"I am utterly dependent upon him—we all are; I am living upon his generosity and you, yourself, are dependent upon him."

"In other words you have already sold me to him?"

"No, he has bought us all."

"Therefore, I belong to him already whether I want to or not?"

"He does not demand that. He asks for nothing, demands nothing."

"How generous!"

"Julia!"

"Yes, yes, I understand! Tell him that so far as I'm concerned he can come whenever he pleases."

She began to tremble as she spoke. Who was it that had really said that? Was it she? No, rather another being concealed within her who tyrannized over her.

"Thank you, my child, thank you!"

The father rose to embrace his daughter; but she, pushing him aside, cried out:

"No, don't soil me!"

"But, my dear child . . ."

"Go and kiss your mortgages! Or rather the ashes of those that would have cast you into prison."

*   *   *

"Julia, didn't I tell you that Alejandro Gomez knows how to get what he wants? To say such things to me! To me!"

These were the first words which the young

"Indian" addressed to Victorino's daughter. The young girl trembled at them; for the first time in her life she sensed that she was standing before a real man. And it seemed to her that this man was more docile and less uncouth than she had expected.

At the third visit the parents left them alone. Julia trembled. Alejandro remained silent. For a time this trembling and this silence persisted.

"Julia, you seem to be ill," he said.

"No, no, I'm all right."

"Then, why do you tremble so?"

"Perhaps because of the cold."

"No, because you're afraid."

"Afraid! Afraid of what?"

"Afraid of me."

"Why should I be afraid of you?"

"Yes, you're afraid of me."

And she gave vent to her fear by bursting into tears. Julia wept from the very depths of her being—wept with all her heart. Her sobs choked her, she could not breathe.

"Am I an ogre?" whispered Alejandro.

"They have sold me! They have sold me! They have bartered my beauty! They have sold me!"

"Who says so?"

"I, I say so! But no—I'll never be yours, not unless I'm dead."

"You will be mine, Julia; you will give your-self to me and you will love me . . . Do you mean that you're not going to love me? Me? Well, that's the last straw!"

There was something in the tone of that "me" that shut off the fountain of Julia's tears: her heart seemed to stop beating. Then, as she looked at this man, a voice seemed to say: "This is a *man*."

"You can do with me whatever you please," she said.

"What do you mean by that?" he asked, continuing to address her with the familiar "tu" (thou).

"I don't know . . . I don't know what I mean . . ."

"Why do you say that I can do whatever I want with you?"

"Because you can . . ."

"What I want," and his *I* sounded clear and triumphant, "is to make you my wife."

Julia was unable to suppress a cry; her large beautiful eyes shone in surprise as she gazed at the man who was smiling and thinking to himself: "I shall have the most beautiful wife in all Spain."

"But what did you think I wanted?" he asked her.

"I thought . . . I thought . . ."

Again her breast heaved with stifled sobs. Presently she felt lips pressing upon hers and heard a voice that was saying to her:

"Yes, my wife . . . mine . . . my own . . .

my legitimate wife of course. The law will sanction my will . . . or my will the law!"

"Yes, yours."

She was conquered. And so the wedding was arranged.

*   *   *

What was there about this crude and secretive man that frightened her while compelling her respect? And the most horrible thing about it was that he inspired in her a sort of strange love. For Julia did not want to love this adventurer, who had made up his mind to have one of the most beautiful of women for his wife simply to make her show off his millions. But, unwilling to love him, she felt herself yielding to a submission that bore some resemblance to passion. It was akin to that form of love that an arrogant conqueror must inspire in the heart of a captive slave-girl. He had not purchased her, no! but he had conquered her.

"But," said Julia to herself, "does he really love me? Does he love me, really me, as he says he does—and how he says it! Does he love me, or does he seek only to display my beauty? Can I mean nothing more to him than a rare and costly piece of furniture? Is he truly in love with me? Won't he soon become tired of my charms? At any rate he's going to be my husband and I'll see myself free from this cursed home, free from my father. For my father shall certainly not live with us! We will give him an allowance and let him continue insulting my poor mother and carrying on his intrigues with servant girls. We shall avoid his getting into business difficulties again. And I shall be wealthy, enormously wealthy!"

But this did not satisfy her completely. She knew that she was envied by the townspeople; she knew that her wonderful good-fortune was the favorite topic of conversation and that it was said that her beauty had won for her all that it possibly could. But did this man love her? Did he truly love her?

"I must win his love," she would say to herself. "I must have him really love me—I cannot become his wife if he does not, for that would be a transaction of the worst possible kind. But, do I really love him?" In his presence, she felt herself grow timid, as a mysterious voice, issuing from the depths of her being, said to her: "This is a real man." Every time Alejandro said *I* she would tremble. She trembled with love although she thought it was for some other reason, or else was totally ignorant of its cause.

*　　*　　*

They were married and went to live in the capital. Thanks to his large fortune Alejandro had numerous acquaintances and friends but they were somewhat curious. Julia imagined that most of the people who frequented their home, and there were many aristocrats among them, were debtors of her husband who loaned them money on solid mortgages. But she knew nothing concerning his affairs, and he never spoke to her about them. There was nothing that Julia did not have; she was able to gratify her slightest whim, but she missed something which, indeed, it was natural that she would desire. It was no longer the love of this man who she felt had conquered and even bewitched her, but rather the absolute certainty of that love that she desired. "Does he love me or doesn't he?" she would ask herself. "He showers me with attentions, he treats me with the greatest respect, but a trifle as if I were only a capricious child; he even spoils me. But does he really love me?" It was quite useless to speak of love and affection to this man.

"Only fools talk about such things," he would say. "My charming one . . . my beauty

. . . my beloved . . . I? I talking of such things? Sentiment belongs in novels. I know that you used to enjoy reading them . . ."

"I still like to."

"Then read all you want. Why look here, if it pleases you, I will erect a pavilion on the grounds next door, which you can use as a library and I will stock it with all the novels that have been written since the time of Adam."

"How you talk!"

Alejandro dressed as modestly and carelessly as possible. It was not so much that he sought to pass unnoticed because of his attire, but he affected a certain plebeian vulgarity. It was hard for him to change his clothes, since he had grown fond of those he was accustomed to wearing. One would have said that whenever he donned a new suit he purposely rubbed himself against the walls to make it appear shabby. On the other hand, he insisted that his wife should dress herself most elegantly, in a

manner that would show her natural beauty
off to the best advantage. He paid all his bills
promptly but those that he paid most cheerfully
were the accounts of the dressmakers and the
modiste for fluffs and frills for his Julia.

He took pleasure in going out with her and
in emphasizing the difference in dress and
bearing that existed between them. It amused
him to notice that men stopped to glance at
his wife, and if she in turn coquettishly pro-
voked their glances, he did not notice it, or
else pretended not to. He seemed to be saying to those who looked at her with sensual
desire: "She pleases you? Well, I'm most
delighted, but she's mine, mine only, so
you can covet all you want!" She guessed this
sentiment and thought: "Does this man love
me or doesn't he?" For always she thought of
him as *this man*—as *her man* or rather, as the
man whose mistress she had become. Little by
little she developed the soul of a slave-girl in

164

a harem; a favorite, unique slave, but a slave-girl just the same.

No intimacy existed between them. She could not imagine what might interest her husband. Once she ventured to ask him about his family.

"My family?" Alejandro replied. "I have no family but you. I am my family. I and you who are mine."

"But what of your parents?"

"You must realize that I never had any. My family begins with me. I made myself."

"I wanted to ask you something else, Alejandro, but I don't dare."

"What do you mean you don't dare? Am I going to devour you? Have I ever taken offense at anything you have said to me?"

"No, never, I have no complaint to make ..."

"Well, that's the last straw!"

"I have no complaint to make, but . . ."

"Good, ask it and let's have it over with."

"No, I'm not going to ask you."

"Ask me!"

And he said it in such a tone and with such supreme egoism that she answered him in a voice trembling with fear and love—the submissive love of a favorite slave:

"Well, then, tell me, are you a widower?"

"Yes, I am a widower."

"And your first wife?"

"People have been telling you something."

"Why, no, but . . ."

"People have been telling you something; what is it?"

"Well, yes, I heard something . . ."

"And you have believed it?"

"No . . . No, I didn't believe it."

"Of course you couldn't have—you shouldn't have believed it."

"And I didn't believe it."

"That's quite natural. Anyone who loves me as you love me and who belongs to me as you do, could not believe such fantastic lies."

"It's evident that I love you," and as she said this she hoped to excite a similar avowal of affection on his part.

"I have already told you that I don't like phrases from sentimental novels. The less one confesses one's love for another, the better it is."

After a short pause he continued:

"They have told you that I was married in Mexico, when I was very young, to an immensely wealthy woman, much older than I— an old heiress—and that I forced her to make me her heir, and then killed her. That's what they've told you, isn't it?"

"Yes, that's what they told me."

"And did you believe it?"

"No, I didn't believe it. I could not believe that you killed your wife."

"I see that you have more sense than I gave you credit for. How could I have killed my own wife—something belonging to me?"

What was it that made poor Julia tremble when she heard this? She did not realize the cause of her trembling—but it was the word *thing* applied to his former wife by her husband.

"It would have been absolutely foolish," Alejandro went on. "What for? To be her heir? Why, I enjoyed her fortune as much then as I do today! To kill one's own wife! There's no reason in the world for killing one's own wife."

"Nevertheless, there have been husbands who have killed their wives," Julia ventured to say.

"For what reason?"

"Through jealousy or infidelity . . ."

"Nonsense! Only fools are jealous. Only fools can be jealous because fools alone permit their wives to be untrue to them. But I! My wife can't possibly deceive me. My first one couldn't and neither can you!"

"Don't talk like that. Let's change the subject."

"Why?"

"It pains me to hear you say such things. As if the thought of deceiving you could enter my brain, even in dreams . . ."

"I know; I knew it even without your telling me so: I know that you will never be untrue to me! Deceive me! My own wife? Impossible. As for her, the other one, she died without my having killed her."

This was one of the times when Alejandro spoke at greatest length to his wife. She had remained pensive and trembling. Did this man love her or didn't he?

* * *

Poor Julia! This new home of hers was terrible; as terrible as her father's. She was free, absolutely free. She was able to do whatever she fancied there, go and come at will, receive her women-friends and even men as she pleased. But her lord and master—did he love her?

This uncertainty of his love held her a captive in this magnificent prison with wide-open doors.

A ray of a rising sun filtered through the tempestuous shadows of her captive soul when she realized that she was pregnant by her husband. "Now," she said, "I shall know if he loves me."

When she announced the good news to her husband he exclaimed:

"I expected it. Now I have an heir and I will make a man of him—a man like me. I expected him."

"And what if he hadn't come?" she inquired.

"Impossible! He had to come. I had to have a child—I."

"Well, a great many people who marry don't have any."

"Perhaps others don't. But not I! I had to have a child."

"And why so?"

"Because you couldn't do otherwise than bear one."

The child was born, but the father remained as uncommunicative as ever. Only he forbade his wife to nurse the boy.

"I don't doubt that you are healthy and strong, but nursing mothers lose their strength, and I don't want you to. I want you to keep yourself young as long as possible."

He relinquished the idea only after the doctor had assured him that Julia, far from being hurt, would be benefited by nursing her child, and that her beauty would thereby reach its plenitude.

The father refused to kiss his child. "One only annoys them with such tender foolishness," he would explain. Occasionally he would take him up in his arms and examine him attentively for a long time.

"Didn't you once question me about my family?" said Alejandro one day to his wife.

"Well, here it is. Now I have a family and some one who will be my heir and continue my work."

Julia was tempted to ask her husband what his work was, but she did not dare. "My work!" Indeed, what could the work of this man be? She had heard him use this same expression before.

Among the people who came most frequently to the house were the Count and Countess of Bordaviella and, especially, the Count who had business relations with Alejandro and to whom the latter had loaned considerable sums on interest. Often the Count would play a game of chess with Julia, who liked it, and unburden his mind by confiding to his friend—his creditor's wife—his unfortunate domestic affairs. For the hearth of the Count of Bordaviella was a diminutive hell, without very much flame, however. The Count and Countess did not get along nor did they love each other.

Both of them devoted themselves to their own interests and she, the Countess, made herself liable to outrageous gossip. People had invented for her benefit this little riddle: "Who is Count of Bordaviella's assistant husband?" So it was that the Count went to the home of the beautiful Julia, to play chess with her and to contrive another's misfortune to console him for his own.

"What? Has that Count been here today, too?" demanded Alejandro of his wife.

"That Count . . . that Count . . . why, what Count do you mean?"

"What one! The Count! There is only one Count, one Marquis and one Duke . . . To me they're all the same, as if they were one and the same thing."

"Well, yes; he has been here."

"I'm glad, if it amuses you. That's the only thing he's good for—the poor fool."

"Well, I think that he's an intelligent man,

cultured, well brought up and very attractive."

"Yes, like those men you read about in novels. But if that interests you . . ."

"And he's so very miserable."

"Bah! That's his own fault."

"Why?"

"Because he's such an idiot. What happens to him is perfectly natural. It is quite natural that a wife should deceive a little bungler like this Count. Why, he's not a man! I don't know how any one could have married such a thing as that. Of course, she didn't marry him but his title. I would like to see a woman treat me as his woman treats that miserable creature!"

Julia looked at her husband and suddenly exclaimed, without realizing what she was saying:

"And what if she should? What if your wife should turn out as this woman has?"

"Nonsense!" and Alejandro burst into laugh-

ter. "You are trying to season our domestic life
with the salt extracted from books. But if you
want to test me by making me jealous you're
making a mistake. I'm not of that kind.
Amuse yourself playing with the poor fool."

"Is it possible that this man is entirely free
from jealousy?" Julia asked herself. "Doesn't
it trouble him to see the Count coming to my
home and courting me as he does? Is it his
confidence in my fidelity and my love? Or is
it his confidence in his power over me? Is it
mere indifference? Does he or does he not
love me?" She began to grow exasperated.
Her lord and master was torturing her heart.

The unfortunate woman persisted in trying
to provoke her husband's jealousy as if it were
the touchstone of his love; but she did not succeed.

"Do you want to accompany me to the
Count's?" she would ask.

"What for?"

"To take tea."

"Tea? I have no stomach ache. In my time, where I come from, we only drink this dirty water when we have a stomach ache. May it agree with you! And do your best to console the poor Count a little. I suppose the Countess will be there with her latest flame. That's fine society!"

* * *

Meanwhile, the Count continued to besiege Julia. He pretended to suffer from his domestic misfortunes in order to arouse his friend's compassion and, through her compassion, to lead her into love, into illegitimate love. At the same time he sought to make her understand that he was also somewhat aware of the little troubles in her own household.

"Yes, Julia, it's true; my house is hell, a perfect hell!—you do right to pity me as you do. Ah! if we had only known each other sooner!

Before I had joined myself to my misfortune.
And before you . . ."

"And I to mine, you mean to say?"

"No, no, that's not what I meant . . ."

"Well, what was it that you intended to say,
Count?"

"Before you had given yourself to this other
man, to your husband . . ."

"And are you so certain then that I would
have given myself to you?"

"Oh, of course, beyond a doubt."

"How insolent you men are!"

"Insolent?"

"Yes, insolent. I suppose you think you're
irresistible?"

"I?"

"Well who then?"

"Will you allow me to say something to you,
Julia?"

"You may say anything you wish."

"Well, then, it is not I who would have

been irresistible, but my love. Yes, my love!"

"But is this a formal proposal, Count? Don't forget that I am a married woman, virtuous and in love with my husband . . ."

"Oh! as to that . . ."

"Do you presume to doubt it? Yes, I am in love, just what you hear—sincerely in love with my husband . . ."

"But, as for him . . ."

"What do you mean? Who has told you he doesn't love me?"

"You yourself."

"I? When did I tell you that Alejandro does not love me? When?"

"You have told me so with your eyes, with your gestures, with your bearing."

"Now I see that I have been encouraging you to make love to me. Take care, Count, this visit is the last one you will pay me."

"For God's sake, Julia!"

"Yes, that's final, the very last one!"

"For God's sake, Julia! Let me come to see you in silence. Just let me look at you and let me dry, as I behold you, the tears I shed within me . . ."

"How nice!"

"And as for that what I said to you that seemed to offend you so . . ."

"That seemed to? It did offend me . . ."

"Could I offend you?"

"Why, sir!"

"What I said to you that offended you so was only this: That if we had only met—I, before I had delivered myself into my wife's hands and you into your husband's,—I should have loved you as madly as I love you now. Let me bare my heart to you! I should have loved you as madly as I love you now. My love would have won your love. Julia, I am not one of those men who seek to conquer and domi-ate a woman by their own worth—for what they are—who demand that they be loved without giving their affection in turn. You won't find such pride in my make-up."

Julia was absorbing the poison drop by drop.

"There are some men," continued the Count, "who are incapable of loving but who demand that they be loved and who think they have the right to the affection and absolute fidelity of the poor woman who has yielded herself to them. They select a woman who is famous for her beauty in order to glorify themselves and lead her along beside them like a tame lioness. 'Look at my lioness,' they exclaim; 'you see how she has been conquered by me'! And that's why they love their lionesses."

"Count, Count! You are entering upon a subject . . ."

The Count of Bordaviella drew still nearer, almost to her ear. He made her feel the tremor of his gasping breath against the lovely shell of pink flesh that lay among those shimmering locks of auburn hair, as he whispered:

"Julia, it is your soul I am entering."

His familiar "thou" made the guilty ear blush.

Julia's bosom rose and fell like the ocean at the approach of a storm.

"Yes, Julia, I'm entering your soul!"

"Leave me alone, for Heaven's sake leave me alone! What if he should come in!"

"He won't come in. He is not interested in anything you do. He leaves us here alone like this because he doesn't love you . . . No, no, he doesn't love you, he doesn't love you, Julia, he doesn't love you!"

"It is because he has absolute confidence in me . . ."

"In you? No, in himself. He has an absolute, blind faith in himself! He thinks that he, because he is what he is—Alejandro Gomez, the man who made his own fortune, I won't say how—he thinks that he could not be deceived by a woman. He despises me—I know!"

"Yes, he despises you . . ."

"I knew it! But he despises you just as much as he despises me."

"For Heaven's sake keep quiet. You are killing me . . ."

"He is the one who will kill you—he, your husband. And you won't have been the first one, either!"

"That is an infamy, Count, an infamy! My husband did not kill his wife! Go away from here; go away and don't ever return!"

"I'll go, but I shall come back. You will send for me."

With this he took his departure, leaving her wounded to the very heart.

"Can this man have spoken the truth?" she asked herself. "Can it be so? He revealed to me what I did not wish to confess even to myself. Can it be true that he despises me? Can it be true that he does not love me?"

* * *

Rumors were beginning to be spread among the scandal-mongers of the capital concerning Julia's relations with the Count of Bordaviella. Alejandro didn't hear anything of them, or else he pretended not to. He cut short the veiled insinuations which a friend had begun to make to him by saying: "I know what you are going to tell me. But stop; these tales are but idle gossip. One must let romantic women interest themselves." Could he—could he be a coward?

But one day at the Casino when some one in front of him had taken the liberty of making an ambiguous jest with a double meaning about horns, he picked up a bottle and hurled it at the man's head. A terrible scandal had resulted.

"To me—to me he comes with such jokes!" he exclaimed in his most restrained tone of voice. "As if I did not understand him! As if I didn't know the idiotic things that are passed around, among busy-bodies, concerning my poor wife's romantic whims! I am determined to tear these unfounded stories up by the roots . . ."

"But not like that, Don Alejandro," some one ventured to tell him.

"How then? Tell me how."

"You would do better to destroy the cause of the tales."

"Oh! indeed. By closing my door to the Count?"

"That would be the wiser course."

"But that would be justifying the slanderers. Besides I am not a tyrant. If this puppet of a Count amuses my poor wife, am I going to deprive her of the distraction afforded by this idiot who is—I swear—a thorough simpleton, an inoffensive nonentity who's trying to play the rôle of a Don Juan—merely because the other idiots will say this or that about it? Well, that's the last straw! Fancy my wife

184

deceiving me! Me! You don't know me."

"But Don Alejandro, what about appearances . . .?"

"I live by realities and not appearances!"

The following day two very serious looking gentlemen presented themselves at Alejandro's home to demand satisfaction of him in the name of the insulted man.

"Tell him," he said to them, "to send me his doctor's or his surgeon's bill; I will pay it as well as whatever other damages there may have been."

"But Don Alejandro . . ."

"Well, what do you want?"

"We ask nothing. But the offended party demands reparation . . . some satisfaction . . . an honorable explanation . . ."

"I don't understand you . . . or rather I don't care to understand."

"And if not, then he demands a duel."

"Very well. Whenever he wishes. But it is

quite unnecessary for you to bother about arrangements. We have no need of seconds. Just tell him that he can notify me when his head is better—I mean when he has recovered from the bottle-blow; we will go anywhere he wishes, lock ourselves in a room and settle this affair properly with our bare fists. I agree to no other weapons. He'll see who Alejandro Gomez is."

"But you are making fun of us, Don Alejandro," cried one of the seconds.

"Not at all. You are of one world, I of another. You come from illustrious fathers— from aristocratic families . . . As for me I have only the one family I have made for myself. I come from nothing at all and I don't want to hear about such hypocrisies as a code of honor. So there, you know my stand."

The seconds rose to their feet and one of them, very gravely and with a certain emphasis, but not wholly disrespectfully (for after all

186

this person was an influential millionaire and a man of mysterious birth), exclaimed:

"In this case, Señor Don Alejandro Gomez, allow me to tell you . . ."

"Say anything you want, but be careful of your words, for I have another bottle handy."

"Then, Señor Don Alejandro Gomez," he said raising his voice, "you are not a gentleman."

"Why, of course not; of course I'm not a gentleman. I, a gentleman? Since when? How? I was brought up an ass-keeper and not a gentleman! And I didn't even bring lunch to the man who called himself my father, riding upon a donkey, but walking on foot. Of course I'm no gentleman. Gentlemanliness and me—come now, how absurd!"

"Let's leave," said the other witness, "we have nothing further to do here. And as for you, Señor Don Alejandro, you will have to stand the consequences of your incomprehensible conduct."

"Certainly, I await them. And as for that—that gentleman with a loose tongue whose skull I have fractured—tell him, I repeat it, to send me the doctor's bill and in the future to be careful of what he says. And you two, for anything can happen, if one day you find yourselves in need of this savage and incomprehensible millionaire, a savage who has no code of honor, you can turn to me for assistance and I will serve you as I have served and still do serve other gentlemen."

"This is unbearable! Let's leave!"

With these words the seconds made their departure.

* * *

That same night Alejandro told his wife about the scene he had had with the two seconds, after having explained to her the affair of the bottle. He amused himself greatly in telling about his adventure. She listened to what he had to say with terror.

"I, a gentleman! Alejandro Gomez! Never! I am only a man, but I am a real man."

"And what about me?" she asked, in order to say something.

"You? You are a real woman. A woman who reads novels. And he, the little Count, who plays chess with you, is a nobody, less than a nobody. Why should I forbid you to amuse yourself with him as you might with a little lap-dog? If you were to purchase one of those fuzzy little dogs, or an angora cat, or a little pet monkey, and you were to pet and even kiss it, would I then take the little dog, or the cat or the pet monkey and throw it out of the window? That would be a clever thing to do, especially when it might fall on the head of some passer-by! Well, it's the same with that Count, another little puppy or kitten or monkey as he is! Amuse yourself with him as much as you please!"

"But, Alejandro, they are right about what they say; you must close your house to this man . . ."

"Man, did you say?"

"As you like. But you should close your door to the Count of Bordaviella."

"Why don't you? As long as you don't there's precious little he has won in your heart. For if you had begun to take an interest in him you would have sent him away just to protect yourself!"

"And what if I were interested in him?"

"That's a good one! Here we are back at the same point again. You want to make me jealous! Me! When will you realize that I am not like other men?"

*   *   *

As time passed Julia understood her husband less and less, but he fascinated her more and more, and she felt more anxious than ever to know if he really loved her or not. On the other hand, Alejandro, although he felt fully reassured as to his wife's fidelity or rather as to the impossibility of his wife's—Alejandro's wife —deceiving him, a real man! began to say to himself: "This life here in the capital and all these novels she reads is turning my poor wife's head." He therefore decided to take her away to the country and so they departed for one of their estates.

"A short stay in the country will do you a lot of good," he said to her. "It calms one's nerves. Furthermore, if you are afraid of being bored without having your little monkey you can invite him to accompany us. Because now you know that I am not jealous. I am very sure of you, of my wife."

But poor Julia's anxiety only increased in

the country. She was frightfully bored. Her husband would not allow her to read.

"I brought you here to take you away from your books and to cure you of your neurasthenia before it became worse."

"My neurasthenia?"

"Why, yes! That's all that's the matter with you. It comes from the books you read."

"Then I will never read any more of them."

"I don't ask that of you . . . I demand nothing. Am I some kind of a tyrant? Have I ever exacted anything of you?"

"No, you don't even demand that I love you."

"Naturally, when that's something it would be impossible to demand! And besides, I know that you love me and that it is impossible for you to love any one else . . . Since you have known me and learned, thanks to me, what a real man is like, you are quite incapable of loving another man even if you set out to. But enough of this book-talk. I have told you that

I don't like novels. They're just the thing to serve as the topic of conversation with little Counts over the tea-table."

Julia's suffering increased when she discovered that her husband was involved in a common love affair with a coarse servant girl who was not even pretty. One night when they were alone together after dinner, Julia suddenly said to him:

"Don't think, Alejandro, that I have not noticed your affair with Simona."

"Nor have I tried to conceal it. But it is of no importance. Chicken every day . . ."

"What do you mean by that?"

"That you are much too beautiful for daily use."

His wife trembled. It was the first time that her husband had ever referred to her openly as beautiful. Could he possibly love her?

"But," said Julia, "with that bundle of rags!"

"For that very reason! Her dirtiness amuses

me. Don't forget that I was brought up in a sort of pig pen and that I am fairly susceptible to what one of my friends calls the voluptuousness of dirt. And now, after a taste of this little rustic appetizer I shall appreciate all the more your beauty, your elegance and your refinement."

"I hardly know whether you are flattering or insulting me."

"There now! Your neurasthenia again! And I had thought you were improving!"

"Of course, you men can gratify your every whim and deceive us . . ."

"Who has deceived you?"

"You!"

"Do you call that deceiving you? Bah! Books . . . books! I wouldn't give a pin for Simona . . ."

"Of course not. She is nothing more than a little puppy, a little kitten or a pet monkey to you!"

"Yes, a pet monkey, that's it. Nothing more than a pet monkey. That's what she looks like most! You certainly named her well: a monkey! But does that mean that I have ceased to be your husband?"

"You mean that I have not ceased to be your wife because of this affair . . ."

"I see, Julia, you are getting clever . . ."

"One acquires everything in time."

"From me, of course, and not from your little pet monkey."

"Of course, from you."

"Good. I can't believe that this little rustic incident is going to make you jealous. You, jealous! You, my wife! And of this she-monkey? As for her, I give her a dowry and that's the end!"

"Of course, when one is wealthy . . ."

"And with this dowry she'll get married in a jiffy and present her husband with a boy along with her dowry. And should the boy resemble his father, who is a real man, it will be a double gain for her sweetheart."

"Be still! Be still!" and poor Julia burst into tears.

"I thought," concluded Alejandro, "that country life had cured you of your neurasthenia. Be careful or it will get worse!"

Two days later they returned to their city residence.

* * *

Julia resumed her suffering and the Count of Bordaviella resumed his visits, although with greater prudence than before. It was finally Julia who, exasperated, began to listen to the venomous insinuations of her friend and especially to make a show of this friendship before her husband who limited himself to a single warning: "We will have to return to the country and submit you to treatment."

One day, exasperated beyond all endurance, Julia attacked her husband, saying:

"You're not a man, Alejandro, no; you're not a man!"

"What's that! I? And why not?"

"No, you're not a man, you're not!"

"Explain yourself."

"Now I know that you don't love me, that nothing that concerns me interests you, that to you I am not even the mother of your child and that you only married me out of vanity to boast of it, to exhibit me, to exalt yourself by my beauty, to . . ."

"Well, well, that's more literature. Why am I not a man?"

"Now I know that you don't love me."

"I've told you a hundred times already that all this talk about loving and not loving, about love and all that nonsense, is conversation fit for some Count's tea-table."

"Now I know that you don't love me."

"Well, what else?"

"But your consenting that the Count—the monkey, as you call him—should enter here whenever he pleases . . ."

"You are the one who consents to that."

"And why shouldn't I consent to it, if he is my lover? Now you've heard it! He is my lover."

Alejandro remained impassive, looking at his wife. The latter expecting an outburst of rage from the man, became more excited than before and shouted at him:

"Well, what? Aren't you going to kill me now as you did the other woman?"

"It is not true that I killed the other woman and it is equally untrue that this monkey is your lover. You are lying to me in order to provoke me. You want to make an Othello out of me and my home is not a theater. Furthermore, if you continue this way, you will end by becoming insane and we shall have to shut you up."

"Insane? I—insane?"

"Absolutely! Fancy reaching the point of believing she has a lover! That is to say, trying to make me believe it! As if my wife could deceive me! Me! Alejandro Gomez is no monkey. He's a real man! But you won't succeed in your ambition, you won't succeed in having me tickle your ears with story-book words and expressions fit for a Count's tea-table conversations. My home is not a theater."

"Coward, coward, coward that you are!" screamed Julia, quite beyond herself.

"We shall have to use special measures," retorted her husband.

And he went off.

*   *   *

Two days after this scene, after having kept his wife under lock and key, Alejandro sum-

moned her to his study. Poor Julia was terrified. She found her husband awaiting her
in his office with the Count of Bordaviella and
two other gentlemen.

"Listen, Julia," said her husband with a
terrible calm, "these two gentlemen are alienists who have come here at my request to examine your case in order that we may be able
to give you the proper treatment. You are not
very well mentally; doubtless you are aware of
this during your moments of lucidity."

"And what are you doing here, Juan?" Julia
asked the Count, without noticing her husband.

"You see?" exclaimed the latter, turning toward the doctors. "She persists in her hallucination. She insists on imagining that this
gentleman is . . ."

"Yes, he is my lover!" she broke in. "If it
is not true, then let him deny it."

The Count looked fixedly at the floor.

"You see, Count, how she persists in her madness," said Alejandro to Bordaviella. "Indeed you have never had—you could not have had any relationship of this nature with my wife . . ."

"Of course not!" cried the Count.

"You see how it is?" continued Alejandro, addressing the doctors.

"But how do you dare, Juan, you, my darling, deny that I have belonged to you?" cried Julia.

The Count trembled beneath Alejandro's frigid gaze and he replied:

"Control yourself, Señora. You know quite well that if I frequented your house it was solely as your friend, Señora, yours and your husband's, and also that I, a Count of Bordaviella, could never have offended a friend such as . . ."

"Such a friend as I am," interrupted Alejandro. "I! I? Alejandro Gomez! No Count could offend me, any more than my wife could betray me. So you see, gentlemen, the unfortunate woman is quite insane."

"And you, too, Juan, you too, my darling!" she cried. "Coward, coward that you are! My husband has threatened you and because you're afraid, you coward, you don't dare tell the truth, and so you're lending your aid to this infamous farce to declare me insane! Coward! Coward! Villain—you, yes, and my husband, too!"

Poor Julia was overcome by a nervous fit and fainted dead away.

"And now, my dear sir," said Alejandro to the Count, "we shall leave the room and allow these two excellent doctors to finish their consultation alone with my poor wife."

The Count followed him. When they were out of the room Alejandro said to him:

"So then you thoroughly understand, Count, either my wife is declared insane or I will blow out your brains and hers, too. It is up to you to decide."

"The thing for me to do is to pay you what I owe in order to have no further dealings with you."

"No! What you owe me is to keep your mouth shut. So we have decided—my wife is raving mad and you are the worst of idiots. And—beware of this!" And he showed him a revolver.

When a few minutes later, the two alienists left Alejandro's study, they were saying to each other:

"This is a horrible tragedy. What shall we do?"

"What shall we do but declare her insane? Otherwise this man will kill her and this poor Count as well."

"But what of our professional duty?"

"Our duty in this instance is to prevent a greater crime."

"Would it not be better to declare Don Alejandro crazy?"

"No, he is not crazy; something else is the matter with him."

"Poor woman! It was horrible to listen to her. What I fear is that she will end by really going crazy."

"Well, by declaring her so, perhaps we shall save her. At any rate, we shall remove her from this house."

Consequently they did declare her insane, and, on the strength of this declaration, her husband had her shut up in a sanatorium.

* * *

A starless night, dense, gloomy and cold settled upon Julia's soul when she found herself a prisoner in this sanatorium. Her only consolation was that they brought her son to see her almost every day. She would gather him in her arms and bathe his little face with her tears. And the poor little boy, although he did not understand why, would cry with her too.

"Ah! my baby, my dear baby!" she would say to him, "if I could only drain from you all your father's blood! For he is your father!"

And when she was alone, the poor woman, feeling herself on the verge of insanity, would say: "But won't I end by really going mad in this place and by convincing myself that my whole affair with this infamous Count was merely a dream and a hallucination? Ah! the coward, yes, the coward that he is! To abandon me like this! To allow them to shut me up in this place! Oh! the little monkey —the little monkey! My husband was right! And why didn't Alejandro kill us both? Ah, no! This is a more terrible vengeance! Why should he kill that cowardly monkey! No, indeed, far better to humiliate him to force him to lie and abandon me. He trembled in my husband's presence, he trembled before him. It is because my husband is a man! And why didn't he kill me? Othello would have killed me! But Alejandro is not an Othello; he is not such a brute as Othello. Othello was an impetuous Moor, but not very intelligent. Alejandro has a powerful mind with which to serve his infernal plebeian pride. No! This man did not need to kill his first wife, he made her die. She died of pure fright at his presence. And me . . .? Does he really love me?"

Here, in this madhouse, she began once more to wring her heart and torture her mind with the painful dilemma; "Does he love me—or doesn't he?" Then she would say to herself: "As for me, I love him madly!"

Finally, through fear of really going crazy, she pretended to be cured by assuring them that her love affair with Bordaviella had only been an hallucination. Her husband was informed of this.

One day they summoned Julia to the sitting room, where her husband was waiting for her. She threw herself at his feet, sobbing:

"Forgive me, Alejandro, forgive me!"

"Get up, Julia," he said, assisting her to her feet.

"Forgive me!"

"Forgive you? Forgive you for what? They have told me that you are cured, that you do not have any more of these hallucinations . . ."

Julia observed with terror her husband's cold and penetrating eyes. She was overcome by a mad and blind love, founded upon an equally blind terror.

"You are quite right, Alejandro, you are quite right. I have been quite crazy, absolutely crazy. And to make you jealous, just to make you jealous, I invented all those stories. But they were nothing but lies. Indeed, how could I have deceived you! I, you? Do you believe me now?"

"Once, Julia," said her husband in an icy voice, "you asked me if it were true that I had killed my first wife and I in turn asked you whether you could believe it. What was it that you replied?"

"That I did not believe it; that I could not believe it."

"Well, then, I now say to you that I have never believed—that I could not believe, that you had given yourself to that little monkey. Does this suffice you?"

Julia was trembling, she felt herself on the brink of insanity—of a madness of terror and love combined.

"And now," added the poor woman, kissing her husband and whispering in his ear, "now, Alejandro, do tell me, do you love me?"

Then the poor woman saw in Alejandro for the first time something that she had never seen before she discovered the depths of the terrible and reticent soul which this wealthy, self-made man had kept jealously concealed. It was as though a flash of tempestuous light had for an instant illuminated the black, tene-

brous lake of that soul and had caused its sur-
face to shimmer. It was that she saw two tear-
drops in this man's cold eyes as piercing as
daggers. Then he burst forth:

"Do I love you, my dear child, do I love you!
I love you with all my soul, with all my blood
and with all my being, more than my own self!
At first when we were married I didn't. But
now? Now I love you blindly—wildly! I am
yours more than you are mine."

And, kissing her with bestial fury, feverishly,
deliriously, like a madman, he exclaimed
brokenly: "Julia! Julia! my goddess, my
everything!"

She thought that she would go mad again
at the sight of her husband's naked soul.

"Now I should like to die, Alejandro," she
murmured in his ear, letting her head fall upon
his shoulder.

At these words the man seemed to arouse
himself and shake himself from a dream; and,

as if his eyes, which were again cold and piercing, had swallowed their tears, he said:

"This has not happened, Julia. Do you understand? Now you know everything; but I have not said what I said . . . Forget it."

"Forget it?"

"Well, remember it then, but as if you had never heard it!"

"I will be silent."

"You must not repeat it even to your own self."

"I will not, but . . ."

"That will do."

"But for your sake, Alejandro, let me continue for a moment . . . only one moment . . . Do you love me for my own self, just for what I am, even if I belonged to another man? Or is it just because I am something that belongs to you?"

"I have told you that you must forget what I said to you. If you insist, I shall leave you here. I have come to take you away, but you must leave here entirely cured."

"And I am cured!" his wife affirmed vehemently.

Alejandro took his wife home.

* * *

A few days after Julia's return from the sanatorium the Count of Bordaviella received from Alejandro what was not only an invitation, but a command as well, to come and take dinner at his house. This was the letter:

"As you must know, my dear Count, my wife has left the sanatorium completely cured; and since the unfortunate woman offended you gravely during the sad time of her delirium—although with no offensive intent—by supposing you capable of committing an infamy of which, being the perfect gentleman that you are, you were, of course, utterly incapable, I invite you to take dinner with us the day after tomorrow,

Thursday, for I very much desire to give to such a gentleman as you the full satisfaction that you are entitled to. My wife begs you to come and I order you to. For should you not come on that day to receive these apologies and explanations you will suffer the consequences. And, you know what I am capable of doing.

Alejandro Gomez."

The Count of Bordaviella kept the appointment. He was pale, trembling and quite overcome. The dinner was accompanied by the most depressing conversation. They spoke of the greatest frivolities, in the presence of servants, along with the most suggestive and ferocious of Alejandro's jokes. Julia followed her husband's example. After the dessert Alejandro turned to a servant and said: "Bring in the tea."

"Tea!" escaped from the Count's mouth.

"Why certainly, my dear Count," replied the master of the house. "Not that I have a stomach ache, no, it's merely to preserve the proper tone. Tea goes very well with explanations between gentlemen . . ."

Then he turned to the servant and said: "You may go."

The three of them were left alone. The Count was trembling. He did not dare to taste the tea.

"Serve me first, Julia," said her husband. "I will drink first, Count, so as to show you that one can take tea in my house with perfect confidence."

"But I . . ."

"No, Count; although I am not a gentleman, or even less than that, I have not fallen so low. And now my wife wishes to offer you a few explanations."

Alejandro glanced at Julia, and she, very slowly, began to speak in a ghastly voice. She was gloriously beautiful. Her eyes scintillated like lightning flashes. Her words flowed coldly and slowly, but one could fathom that a devouring flame burned beneath them:

"I had my husband invite you here, Count," Julia began, "because I owe you an explanation for having gravely offended you."

"Me, Julia?"

"Don't call me Julia. Yes, you. When I became mad, when I fell madly in love with my husband and was constantly seeking to discover if he really loved me or not, I attempted to accuse you of having seduced me. This was a jealousy and, due to my madness, I was led to accuse you of having seduced me. This was a lie and it would have been but pure infamy on my part had I not been insane. Is this not true, Count?"

"Indeed, it is, Doña Julia . . ."

"Señora de Gomez," corrected Alejandro.

"You must forgive us for what I accused you of when my husband and I called you the 'little monkey.'"

214

"You are excused."

"What I accused you of at that time was a low and infamous act, quite unworthy of such a gentleman as you."

"That's well put," added Alejandro, "very well put. 'A low and infamous act unworthy of a gentleman.'"

"I repeat again, although I can and really should be excused on account of my condition at that time, nevertheless I ask your pardon. Do you excuse me?"

"Yes, yes, I pardon you, I pardon you both," breathed the Count, more dead than alive, and anxious to escape as soon as possible from this house.

"Us both?" interrupted Alejandro. "You have nothing to pardon me for."

"That's true . . . quite true!"

"Come now, calm yourself," said the husband. "I see that you are very nervous. Take another cup of tea. Julia, serve the Count.

215

Would you like to have a bit of linden juice in it?"

"No, no . . ."

"Well, now that my wife has told you what she had to say to you, and that you have forgiven her for her madness, there only remains for me to beg you to be kind enough to honor our house with your visits. After what has occurred you will certainly understand that it would have very bad effects were we to sever our relations. Now that my wife, thanks to the care I have given her, is completely cured, you run no further risk in coming here. And to prove to you the confidence I have in the complete recovery of my wife, I shall leave you here alone; for she might have something to say to you which she does not dare to speak of in front of me, or which delicacy does not permit me to hear."

Alejandro left the room, leaving them facing each other and equally surprised by his conduct.

216

"What a man!" thought the Count.

"He, indeed, is a man!" said Julia to herself.

A heavy silence followed his departure. Julia and the Count did not dare to look at each other. Bordaviella glanced at the door by which the husband had left.

"Don't look at the door that way," said Julia. "You don't know my husband. He is not hiding behind the door to eavesdrop."

"How do I know he is not? He is capable of having brought witnesses along."

"Why do you say that, Count?"

"Do you think that I have forgotten the day when he brought two doctors along to take part in that scene in which he humiliated me as much as he possibly could and committed the crime of having them declare you insane!"

"But it was the truth. If I had not been mad at the time I would never have said, as I did, that you were my lover."

"But . . ."

"But what . . . Count!"

"Do you too want to declare me insane? Do you mean to say, Julia, that you are going to deny . . .!"

"Dona Julia, or Señora de Gomez if you please!"

"Do you mean to say, Señora de Gomez, that, for one reason or another, you did not eventually accept my advances . . . not my advances, but my love?"

"Count!"

"That you finally not only accepted them but became the party who encouraged them and that . . ."

"I have told you, Count, that I was insane. Must I continue repeating this?"

"Do you deny that I was your lover?"

"I repeat to you again that I was insane."

"I cannot remain another instant in this house! Good bye!"

The Count held out his hand to Julia fearing that she would refuse it. But she took it in hers and said to him:

"Now, then, you know what my husband said. You can come here whenever you wish, now that I am, thanks to God and to Alejandro, completely cured, cured of everything, Count. It would have a bad effect were you to stop your visits."

"But Julia!"

"What! Are you going to begin again? Haven't I told you that I was insane?"

"I am the one you and your husband are going to drive crazy . . ."

"You? Drive you crazy! That doesn't strike me as being an easy thing to do . . ."

"That's evident, you call me 'little monkey'!"

Julia burst out laughing. Ashamed and furious, the Count left the house with the firm resolution never to return.

All these spiritual torments shattered poor Julia's life and she became seriously ill; mentally deranged. Now she seemed to be really going mad. She frequently had spells of delirium during which she would call for her husband in the most ardent and passionate words. The man would abandon himself to the painful transports of his wife endeavoring to calm her. "I am yours, yours, all yours," he would whisper in her ear while she, clinging to his neck, would fairly strangle him in her grasp.

He took her away to one of his estates, hoping that the country life would cure her. But the disease was slowly killing her. Something terrible had entered the depths of her being.

When this wealthy man finally realized that death was going to take his wife from him, he was overcome by a cold and obstinate fury. He summoned the very best doctors. "All is hopeless," they would say to him.

"Save her for me," he would answer.

"It is quite impossible, Don Alejandro, quite impossible."

"Save her, I tell you! I will sacrifice all my wealth, all my millions to save her life!"

"It is impossible, Don Alejandro."

"Then I will give my life for hers! Can't you make a blood transfusion? Take all mine and give it to her. Come now, take mine."

"It is impossible, Don Alejandro, quite impossible."

"What do you mean—impossible? I will give all my blood for her, I say!"

"Only God can save her."

"God! Where is God? I have never thought of Him."

Then to Julia, his wife, who was pale but more beautiful than ever—beautiful with the beauty of approaching death—he would say:

"Julia, where is God?" She, looking upwards with her large, blank eyes would say in a low voice:

"He is there . . ."

Alejandro looked at the crucifix that hung at the head of his wife's bed, he took it down and crushing it in his fist he would exclaim: "Save her for me, save her for me and ask me anything, anything, my entire fortune, all my blood, all myself. . ." Julia would look at him and smile. Her husband's blind fury filled her soul with a very sweet light. At last she was really happy! How had she ever doubted that this man loved her?

Life was ebbing from this poor woman drop by drop. She was as cold as marble. Then her husband lay down beside her and embraced her passionately. He wanted to give her all his warmth for the warmth that was leaving her body. He wanted to give her his very breath. He was half crazy. And always she smiled.

"I am dying, Alejandro, I am dying."

"No, you are not dying," he would say to her. "You can't possibly die."

"It isn't possible for your wife to die, is it?"

"No, my wife can't die. I would rather die myself. We'll see, let death come, let it come to me! Let death come to me! Let it come!"

"Oh! Alejandro. I know now that I have not suffered in vain! And to think that I doubted your love!"

"No, I did not love you, no! I have told you a thousand times, Julia, that these foolish love-words are nothing but literary rubbish. No, I did not love you! Love, love! And to think that all these wretches, these cowards who talk about love, allow their wives to die! No, that is not love. I don't love you . . ."

"Well, what then?" she demanded in a very faint voice, seized again by her former dread.

"No, I don't love you . . . I, I, I . . . There is no word!" And he burst into long, tearless sobs like the gasps of death—the agonized moan of suffering and savage love.

"Alejandro!"

In this one feeble cry was all the sorrowful joy of triumph.

"You are not going to die! You can't die; I don't want you to die! Kill me, Julia, but you must live! Come, kill me!"

"Yes, I am dying . . ."

"And I with you! . . ."

"What of the child, Alejandro?"

"Let him die, too! Why should I love him without you?"

"For God's sake, Alejandro, you are mad . . ."

"Yes, I am the one who is mad. I have always been mad, mad because of you, Julia, crazy about you . . . I, the madman . . . Kill me, Julia, and take me with you!"

"If I only could . . ."

"No, no! Kill me, but you must live. Belong to yourself!"

"And you?"

"Me? If I cannot belong to you, I will be death's!"

He pressed her still closer to him, as if to hold her forever.

"Won't you tell me now who you are, Alejandro?" whispered Julia in his ear.

"I? Oh, just a man—the man you have made of me."

This word sounded like a murmur from beyond death, as if come from the shores of life as the craft is sailing off into shadowy waters beyond.

Soon Alejandro felt that his strong arms were holding only a lifeless form. The deathly cold of the great final night seemed to settle upon his soul. He got up and looked at the now rigid and lifeless beauty. He had never seen her look more beautiful. She seemed to be bathed in the radiance of that light filtering down from the eternal dawn which follows after the final night. Greater even than his recollection of this already frozen corpse he sensed his whole life passing before him like a frozen cloud; this life of his which he had concealed from everybody—even from himself. He even went back over the years as far as his terrible childhood days, to the time when he trembled beneath the pitiless blows dealt by the man who passed for his father; back to the time when he cursed at him, and when, one night, exasperated beyond all endurance, he had shaken his fist at a figure of the Christ in his little village church.

He finally left the room, closing the door after him, and went in search of his child. The little boy was a trifle over three years of age. The father took him in his arms and shut himself in with him. He began kissing him frantically and the child, who was not accustomed to his father's kisses, who, indeed, had never received a single kiss from him, and who possibly guessed the savage passion flooding his breast, began to weep.

"Keep quiet, my child, keep quiet. Will you forgive me what I am about to do? Will you forgive me?"

Terrified, the child remained quiet. He looked at his father who was seeking in his eyes, mouth and curls for the eyes, mouth and curls of his lost Julia.

"Forgive me, my child, forgive me!"

He closeted himself alone for an instant in order to set down his final wishes, and then he returned to his wife—or to what had once been his wife.

"My blood for yours," Alejandro said to her as if she could have heard him. "Death has taken you away and now I am going to come and get you!" For an instant he imagined that he saw his wife smile and that she moved her eyes. He began to embrace her, to call her and to whisper terrifying words of tenderness in her ear. But she was quite cold.

When later on, they had to break down the door of the death chamber, they found him with his arms around his wife. He was pale and deathly cold and bathed in the blood that had been drained completely from him.